BIG RAY

BIG RAY

MICHAEL KIMBALL

BLOOMSBURY CIRCUS
LONDON • NEW DELHI • NEW YORK • SYDNEY

First published in Great Britain 2012

Copyright © 2012 by Michael Kimball

The moral right of the author has been asserted

This book is a work of fiction. Certain characters, inspired by real people
known to the author, have been fictionalized for the purposes of this work.
Otherwise names, places and incidents are the product of the author's
imagination and any resemblance to actual organizations, business
establishments, events or locales is entirely coincidental

Bloomsbury Circus is an imprint of Bloomsbury Publishing Plc
50 Bedford Square
London
WC1B 3DP

www.bloomsbury.com

Bloomsbury Publishing, London, New Delhi, New York and Sydney
A CIP catalogue record for this book is available from the British Library

ISBN 978 1 4088 2805 2

10 9 8 7 6 5 4 3 2 1

Typeset by Hewer Text UK Ltd, Edinburgh
Printed and bound in Great Britain by CPI Group (UK) Ltd, Croydon CR0 4YY

For my dead dad

CHAPTER 1

MY FATHER PROBABLY died on January 28, 2005, but I wouldn't know he was dead until a few days later when my sister called to tell me. My father lived alone and nobody else knew he was already dead either.

★

January 29, 2005, would have been my mother and father's forty-fifth wedding anniversary—if my father hadn't died the day before, if my mother hadn't divorced him ten years before that.

★

I turned thirty-eight years old on February 1, 2005, but my father didn't call me to wish me a happy birthday, which was odd because my father called me nearly every day. I realized he hadn't called for the few days before my birthday either, which was also odd, but I thought my father was probably just waiting to call me on my birthday. It wasn't until the next day, February 2, that I realized my father hadn't called me because he was dead.

★

The next evening, I walked into the house and I heard somebody talking. It was my sister leaving a message on the answering machine. I thought she was probably calling me to wish me a happy birthday, but her voice didn't sound right, and I couldn't understand what she was saying. I picked the telephone up and started saying my sister's name. I repeated it until I got her attention. I knew there was something wrong and I was letting her know I was there.

★

I couldn't get my sister to tell me what was wrong. She was crying and I couldn't get her to stop. She was sobbing and then she started saying my name. She was repeating my name. She was getting ready to say something difficult. My sister caught her breath. She told me our father was dead.

★

I don't remember what I said back. I just remember how hot my face felt The skin on my cheeks and my forehead suddenly felt wet. I felt like I was running a fever. I felt like I had gotten very sick very fast and I was going to throw up. My chin started to shake and my eyelids fluttered. My eyes couldn't focus. I remember looking around the room like I didn't know where I was anymore. Maybe my eyes were looking for my father even though my brain knew I was never going to see him again.

★

The rest of that telephone call is difficult to remember. I think I might have said, *No*—as if I was disagreeing with my sister, as if I could have brought my father back to life just by denying he died. Or I might have said, *Oh no*—as if it was some kind of accident that could be fixed and didn't really concern me. The more I think about it, the more I think I said, *Oh no*—which seems so stupid now, so inadequate. I'm sure my father would have been disappointed with my response, if he had known what it was. My father was disappointed with so many things about me.

★

I remember how I wanted to hang up the telephone. I wanted my sister to call back and say something else. I wanted her to sing happy birthday to me.

★

I asked my sister what happened and she said she didn't know. She told me she had spoken with the police and the coroner's office. She would call me back when she knew more.

★

I hung up the telephone and I stood there looking at it on the wall of the kitchen. My wife had come into the kitchen and she was standing next to me. She must have known from the tone of my voice that something was wrong. She put her arms around me and we stood there in the kitchen holding on to each other and not saying anything.

★

I stared at the telephone on the wall. I waited for it to ring again.

★

It was a couple of hours before my sister called back. She told me she would go to the funeral home in the morning. She said there wasn't anything else to do until then. I remember how I just agreed with her. There wasn't anything anybody could do.

★

I went into the bedroom and lay down on the bed. My wife followed me and lay down beside me. My father was dead and it felt like the whole world had changed. My wife held on to me and I lay in bed with a pillow over my face. It was all I could do right then.

4

★

After I found out my father had died, I cried so much that first night my face got puffy, my eyes prickly and dried out. I felt wired with grief and I couldn't sleep. It was physically exhausting to have a dead father.

★

My father's obituary lists February 2, 2005, as the official date of death even though that's just the day my father was found dead. The obituary also notes that my father was a member of the Waverly School Board and that he enjoyed playing cards, hunting, and fishing. It is sad. Those are the most notable things about my father that could be written in an obituary.

The obituary then lists the family that preceded my father in death and the family that survived my father. I'm one of the people who survived.

CHAPTER 2

MY FATHER WAS born on May 3, 1939, in Mason, Michigan. He was born in a rented farmhouse and delivered by one of the neighbors who was a midwife. Ray Harold Carrier was the first child of Ruth and Harold Carrier. He had an older half sister from his mother's first marriage, but he wouldn't find out about her until years later.

★

My father never would have been born if his mother's first marriage hadn't failed and he always said the odds against him being born were large. In the family story, my grandmother's first marriage was to a man whose last name nobody knows. I've looked for it in the public records, but there never was a marriage license filed for Ruth Everett, and I suspect it may not have been a real marriage. It could have been what was called a "country marriage," an unofficial and not uncommon union often found in poor communities like the one my father grew up in.

★

This family story is sketchy in other ways. It is believed the young couple lived on a farm outside the small town of Mason. Supposedly, that farm sustained them through their first year together, during which time the young couple had a child, my father's half sister. Not long after that, the man walked out of their little farmhouse, leaving my grandmother and their child on the farm. The man didn't come home that night or for many more nights after that. My grandmother didn't know what to do besides take care of the baby and wait for the man to come back.

★

One day, late in the afternoon, my grandmother was looking out the kitchen window when she saw two figures walking across the back fields toward the farmhouse. It was the man, her husband, but he had another woman with him—and then there was another man at the front door, a county police officer who handed my grandmother an official-looking document. Supposedly, she was too upset to read what the paper said, but she could tell it was signed and stamped. She had to vacate the premises or be arrested for trespassing. She was allowed to take her clothes and anything else she brought with her to the marriage, but that man and the other woman kept the baby girl. The county police officer walked my grandmother out of the farmhouse, off the property, and she didn't see her child again until more than twenty years later.

★

There was always something a little unbelievable about this family story. It's difficult to believe it happened that way, but I never heard anybody tell a different version. It was the kind of family story that wasn't talked about much and, when it was, it was done in a kind of whisper. We were told we shouldn't repeat any of it.

All we knew was that something pretty bad happened, but nobody was quite sure what. It's possible that even my grandmother didn't know exactly what had happened. Whatever it was, it made the story of my grandmother's life seem confusing and incomplete and she passed on something of that to my father.

*

There is no record of a divorce for a Ruth Everett in the public records of Ingham County. Supposedly, the marriage was annulled and my grandmother moved back into her childhood home with her parents.

*

Years later, my grandmother met my grandfather at a country dance. We were always told my grandfather was a good dancer and my grandmother looked good in a gingham dress.

They got married about three months after that and my father was born about six months after that. We were always told my father was a small baby—that he was premature and nobody expected him to live. Because of this, my grandmother wouldn't let anybody else hold her baby boy for the first few months he was alive. She thought she just had a few hours and then maybe a few days to keep this baby. Everybody was surprised when my father didn't die.

*

The doctor called my father a miracle baby and some people in my family came to believe my grandmother's arms had special powers. My father claimed to remember these first few days of his life and, in particular, how tightly my grandmother held him in her arms.

*

I'm pretty sure none of that about my grandmother's arms and my father being premature is true. I have his birth certificate and his birth weight is listed as 6 pounds, 12 ounces—a pretty healthy weight for 1939.

CHAPTER 3

THERE IS SOMETHING I didn't say about what was going on when I found out my father had died. I left it out because it wasn't about my father exactly. Also, I didn't want to equate a telephone call about my father being dead with this—that night, before my sister called, I had been in a car accident. Now I think the car accident influenced how I felt when I found out my father was dead.

★

Here's what happened: This other car ran through a red light and I pushed down on the brake pedal as hard as I could, but my car still hit the other car. There wasn't anything I could do to stop it from happening. It happened faster than I could think.

★

I wasn't hurt, but I was upset. I got out of my car and looked at the damage. The hood of my car was crumpled and the engine was hissing. I called the police, but they never showed up to take an accident report. Eventually, the other driver and I decided to exchange insurance information. That's when I noticed it was difficult for me to write. I was shaking. I had to hold my writing hand with my other hand just to write down the man's name and the policy number of the insurance company.

*

When my wife came to pick me up from the car accident, I was still shaking. When I got home, I was still shaking. My wife hugged me and tried to hold me still, but it didn't stop. I think the shaking made it feel worse when my sister called and told me our father had died. I think I may have attributed the fear and the shaking from the car accident to the death of my father.

*

For most of my life, I have been afraid of my father. After he died, I was afraid to be a person without a father, but I also felt relieved he was dead. Everything about my father seemed complicated like that.

CHAPTER 4

I HAVE A cracked photograph of my father as a newborn that is a kind of family portrait. My father's parents are standing outside in front of their rented farmhouse surrounded by weeds. My father's mother is holding him against her left hip, but she's leaning her upper body away from him and looking at the camera in a challenging way. My father's father is standing next to them, but he is leaning away from them too—his eyebrows pinched and his upper lip raised in that universal expression of disgust. My father is making two fists and he is wailing at the bright sky above them. None of the people can get away from each other, but they have created as much distance between each other as they can.

★

My father is almost one year old in the next photograph I have of him. In this one, my father's grandmother sits back in a rocking chair while my father stands up on her lap. His grandmother holds him by the waist, her arms out in front of her, and my father looks so pleased with himself for being upright. He's smiling and waving his hand at whoever is taking the photograph. I don't remember ever seeing that kind of happiness on his face after he became my father.

★

The two people in that photograph, they are both dead now. The person taking the photograph, whoever that was, is probably dead too.

★

There aren't any other photographs of my father until he is about four years old. In one photograph, he is standing in a muddy front yard with his little sister, Darlene, who would have been almost three years old then. My father and his sister are both twisting their hands together in front of themselves as if they are nervous about something or afraid of whoever is taking the photograph.

The background of the photograph is framed by the rough clapboard house they lived in. A lot of the details seem to be washed out, but, looking harder, I notice the shape of somebody standing in the doorway of the house, obscured by a screen door. I can't be sure who it is, but I'm guessing that it's my grandmother because I can see the outline of an apron. I can't see her face, but her body seems hesitant and withdrawn.

★

I don't know too much else about my father's early life, those few years during World War II before he went to school. I don't remember my father ever talking about the blackouts or food rations, and, as far as I know, my father's father didn't fight in the war.

★

As I understand it, my father's family was quite poor. They ate the food they grew on the small plot of land they rented with the farmhouse. That food was supplemented with whatever food my grandfather could buy with the little money he made doing odd jobs. That lack of food is the explanation given for why my father was breast-fed until he was six years old.

CHAPTER 5

MY FATHER WAS sixty-five years old when he died—plus eight months, plus three weeks, plus another few days. I can't be exactly sure because my father had been dead for a few days before anybody found him. My father died alone in his one-bedroom apartment and I still feel guilty about the fact that it was probably five days before anybody knew.

★

We found out my father was dead because he hadn't paid his rent. The apartment manager sent one of the maintenance men to check on my father in his apartment. The maintenance man noticed that my father's pickup truck was parked in front and a few newspapers were piled up around the apartment door. The maintenance man listened at the apartment door and heard the television turned up really loud inside.

★

He said he knocked, but my father didn't answer, which the maintenance man thought was odd, which was why he thought something was wrong. The maintenance man didn't know the volume of the television was up so loud because my father didn't hear well, which was only one of the many things that was wrong with him.

★

The maintenance man didn't want to open the door to my father's apartment by himself. He didn't want to be alone if he was going to find my father dead, so he went back to the apartment complex's main office and got the apartment manager to go back to my father's apartment with him. They opened the apartment door together and they saw my father lying on the floor in front of the couch in the living room.

They said it looked like my father had just fallen asleep watching television. They said they called my father's name a few times and he didn't answer them. They noticed that the remote control for the television had fallen out of my father's hand. They said my father wasn't moving and it didn't look like he was breathing. They said there was a smell, but they didn't know whether the smell was from the apartment, which was old for an apartment, or whether the smell was from my father, who was old for a person but not so old that he should have already been dead.

★

The maintenance man and the apartment manager didn't go inside my father's apartment. They closed the apartment door and called the police, who responded not long after that and confirmed that my father was in fact dead. The police said my father had probably been dead for a few days and he probably hadn't been murdered.

★

Based on the unread newspapers, the police guessed that my father died on January 28, 2005. That was the earliest date on any of the newspapers piled up around his apartment door. Of course, the police weren't sure he died on that day. My father could have died the evening of January 27—after he had picked up that day's newspaper. Or it could have been January 29. It's possible my father hadn't opened the apartment door to pick up the newspaper on January 28.

Whenever it was, I'm glad my father didn't die at the beginning of the month. I don't know how long it would have been before somebody found him.

CHAPTER 6

MY FATHER STARTED going to school after the war ended. It was 1945 and he was six years old. His report card from first grade shows he mostly received As and Bs. There is no explanation for why he received a C in citizenship, but he must have done something to earn that grade.

Also, the report card has a section titled "Defects That Might Be Corrected" and his first grade teacher, Miss Joanna North, started to write something there and then crossed it out. That thought is sixty-seven years old, incomplete, and illegible.

★

Just one year later, my father's report card shows mostly Bs and Cs. His second grade teacher, Miss Annie Watkins, notes that he is "inclined to waste time."

My father's grades get worse with each school year, but there aren't any other remarks until his sixth grade teacher, Miss Betty Wiegmann, notes that he is "capable of doing better." These teacher comments on my father's elementary school report cards seem like little bits of evidence for the years that followed, early signs of my father's character.

*

There are a couple of elementary school photos of my father, one from second grade and one from fifth grade. In both of them, my father is wearing a plaid shirt and a stupid haircut. He's trying to smile, but it looks like he hasn't learned how. My father looks like the kind of kid the teacher punished when she didn't know who to blame for trouble.

*

One of the few stories my father ever told me about growing up was about the class bully, a new boy who used to wait for my father and beat him up on the way home from school. As my father told it, the bully was kind of stupid and had been held back a grade, which meant he was a lot bigger and stronger than my father and the other kids.

My father got beat up nearly every day of fourth grade until he asked his little brothers to gang up on the bully with him. They waited for the bully behind the school and used a school-yard trick—one of his little brothers got on his knees behind the bully and then my father pushed the bully so he fell over his little brother. After the bully was down on the playground, my father and his little brothers hit and kicked him until he rolled up into a ball. That was one of the few proud moments of my father's childhood.

*

Another story my father told me was about a stray cat that lived around one of the rented houses where my father grew up. The stray cat had kittens and then, supposedly, the mother cat killed one of the kittens. I doubt that is what actually happened. More likely, the mother cat did what it could to keep its kitten alive, but the kitten died anyway.

Regardless, as my father told it, his father took the mother cat and the kittens down to the river that ran behind their house. My father's father shot the mother cat with a shotgun and then drowned all the kittens that were still alive.

*

That story was why, when I was growing up, I wasn't allowed to have a cat. That was why I also wasn't allowed to have a dog or any other kind of pet—no matter how many times I asked. As some kind of shiny consolation, my parents would buy me glossy photo-books of cats and dogs for my birthdays and Christmas. Sometimes, when I was feeling particularly lonely, I would pull one of the glossy photobooks down from the bookshelf in my bedroom and start naming the cats or the dogs.

*

There is a photograph of my father from when he is about twelve years old. He is holding a fishing pole with one hand and standing in the middle of a dirt road that disappears behind him. He is squinting his eyes against the camera and he doesn't look happy even though his other hand is holding up a string of seven trout he must have caught in the river.

★

There is a photograph of a group of boys standing on some rock cliffs above a swimming hole. Most of them are naked and one of them is crouching, getting ready to jump in the water. One of them must be my father—otherwise, I don't know why he saved the photograph—but all their faces are too far away to see. It's strange, though, my father always used to say he didn't know how to swim.

CHAPTER 7

I FLEW BACK to Michigan for my father's funeral. The first leg of the trip to Houston was on a little commuter airplane. The flight felt jumpy. There was a lot of turbulence. I couldn't tell whether my stomach felt floppy and empty and sick because of the turbulence or because my father was dead.

★

Sometimes in the summer, my father would make us all get in the family car and then he would drive us around on these country roads. All I really remember from those drives is how each of us looked out our own open window—that and how loud the wind could be and how the wind would begin to sting my face after a few miles. Eventually, my father drove the whole family apart, but him being dead brought all of us back together again.

★

In the Houston airport, I bought a Mars bar because I was hungry and because my father liked Mars bars. He used to keep them in the pockets of his sport coats.

I ate the Mars bar, but I couldn't really taste it. It should have been sweet, but it tasted stale. I ate the whole thing anyway. I didn't think to look at the wrapper of the Mars bar until I had finished eating it. The expiration date on the bottom of the wrapper had passed.

★

In the Minneapolis airport, I was the first one at the gate for the flight to Lansing. I called home, but my wife didn't answer. I left a message for her. I sat there in one of those hard airport chairs, a bunch of empty airport chairs surrounding me. What I am trying to say is, right then, I felt really alone.

★

At the Lansing airport, my mother and my sister were waiting for me at arrivals. We drove from the airport to a restaurant that was supposed to have good hamburgers. Meals were one of the few things our family could do together. Eating the food filled in the gaps between us.

★

It was at this meal my mother started talking about how poor my father's quality of life was—how little he could do for himself, how unhappy and sick he had become. It was my mother's attempt to make my sister and me feel better about having a dead father. She suggested that my father's unexpected death was a kind of merciful end.

CHAPTER 8

BY HIGH SCHOOL, my father's grades were mostly Cs and Ds. He was flunking classes like English, Bookkeeping, and Social Studies. His English teacher, Miss Emily Rosenstock, notes that my father "could do much better."

My father could have done much better than he did. I don't know why he didn't try. He didn't have a job or a girlfriend for most of high school. He didn't play any sports or participate in any other extracurricular activities. He wasn't doing anything much besides waiting for high school to be over.

★

As teenagers, my father and some of his friends used to take a quart of grape juice, pour it into mason jars, and then add sugar. They would bury the sealed mason jars at the beginning of the school week and the grape juice fermented by the end of the school week. For my father's high school years, that was the fun most Friday nights.

★

There are three photo-booth photographs of my father from 1956. In each of them, his hair is slicked back and the collar on his jacket is turned up. In each of them, a cigarette is dangling from his mouth and he is looking off to the side. In the first one, his eyebrows are raised as if he's asking a question. In the second one, he looks confused. In the third one, he looks angry.

I showed the strip of photographs to my mother and she said that was what my father looked like when she met him. My mother said, "He looked like James Dean then."

★

I don't know if my father ever realized he was having an unhappy life.

★

For his high school graduation photograph, my father is wearing a jacket and a tie. His skin is as smooth as the glossy finish on the photograph. His hair is parted on the side and slicked back in fins. It's obvious the photograph has been touched up and it is the best my father has ever looked.

*

It's not clear whether my father graduated from Okemos High School in the spring of 1957. His report card from that semester of school is incomplete and there wasn't a high school diploma in any of the papers he kept.

CHAPTER 9

I NEED TO say something else about my father. I don't feel good about this, but the first thing I think about when I think about my father is how fat he was.

*

My father got so big it was difficult for him to move his body. It was difficult for him to get up out of a chair and it was difficult for him to walk after he did get up out of a chair. If my father walked from his apartment to his pickup truck, he had to stop and catch his breath before he pulled himself up into the cab. My father got so fat it was even difficult for him to drive his pickup truck. His belly stuck out so far it pushed against the steering wheel, which made it difficult for him to turn the steering wheel as he drove around street corners. This problem was compounded by the fact that my father's largeness pushed his arms so far away from the steering wheel that he had to sit at an odd angle to reach the steering wheel with just one of his hands. Looking back, I can't believe my father never killed himself or somebody else in a traffic accident.

★

My father was so fat he had to use a long-handled device with a clamp on the end of it to pull his shoes and boots over his feet. He used the same long-handled device or a broom handle he had fashioned with a hook on the end of it to reach anything up high. He had another stick with a kind of cup on the end of it. I'm not sure what that one was for.

My father was so fat he also had various types of these devices in the shower. Even so, there were still parts of his body he could not reach.

★

My father was so fat my arms didn't go all the way around him when I tried to hug him. I have a wingspan of 6'6" and there was a big gap between my hands where they touched his back.

★

My father wasn't always so fat, but my first memories of him are of a big man. People called him Big Ray. When I was a kid, the nickname always seemed like a huge compliment. I would have loved to have been called Big Danny. Being big, getting bigger— that was all I was trying to do when I was a kid. It wasn't until I was older that I realized he was reminded of how fat he was every time somebody called him Big Ray. My father must have hated that.

★

When my father was born, he weighed 6 pounds, 12 ounces. When my father was in the Marines, he weighed about 160 pounds. Not long before my father died, he told me he weighed over 500 pounds. Over the course of his lifetime, my father gained at least 493 pounds. Over the course of my lifetime, my father tripled in size.

★

My father also grew from his newborn length of 21" to 5'10" tall as a full-grown man. A couple of decades passed and then my father started to shrink as he gained more and more weight. All the extra pounds my father carried around with him started to compress his body and, not long before my father died, he was only about 5'6" tall and only when he tried to stand up really straight.

★

About 500 pounds is also the size of the largest kind of lion, a full-grown male. The size of my father could be terrifying. I think that partly defined our relationship.

★

It is important to understand what my father looked like to understand what my father was like.

★

My father was the oldest child in his family—besides his secret half sister. Supposedly, this meant he had to do a lot of the work around the house, especially since his sister was sickly, especially when both of his parents had jobs. Apparently, my father had to fix many of the family meals when he was growing up and everybody else got to eat before he did. This is one of the reasons my mother offered for why my father ate so much as an adult. He was always hungry.

*

When I was a little boy, I remember thinking my father was the biggest man in the whole world. I would look at my skinny arms and skinny legs and find it difficult to imagine how I was ever going to grow up into that size of a person.

Up until I was about six years old, I never saw another person who was any bigger than my father was and that felt like a kind of protection. Then one Saturday afternoon, I saw Andre the Giant wrestling on television. He could pick men up who were the size of my father and spin them over his head. After that, every time I looked at my father I felt kind of disappointed.

*

When I was a teenager, there were at least two times my father went on a diet and lost over 100 pounds in just a few months. Once, it was a liquid diet that involved a lot of chocolate, vanilla, and strawberry protein shakes. The other time, my father could only eat meat and vegetables and nobody else in the family was allowed to eat any of his food no matter how much there was. During these times when he dieted, my father could get so angry it was almost always scary whenever he was at home.

★

My father could get angry if somebody sat in his chair or if somebody read the newspaper before he did.

★

My father could get angry if somebody else ate the last piece of bread at dinner.

★

Once, my father got angry with me because he thought I had mowed the lawn in the wrong direction.

★

Another time, my father got angry with me because he thought my haircut was too short and I couldn't explain why that was the current style.

★

I have no explanation for this one, but there was this one time when my father got angry with me for looking out the window.

★

When my father was at home, I often had no idea what to do or say.

★

My father was so fat that even after he lost over 100 pounds, he was still fat. I don't remember my father ever being a normal-sized father. Also, both times my father lost all that weight, he gained it all back within a year, plus some extra pounds on top of that. Even during these two brief periods, my father was always at least twice as big as me, which always made me feel inadequate.

★

Once, when I was ten years old and my father was yelling at me, I called him fat. We all knew he was fat, but I don't remember anybody else ever saying it to him. It was the first time I ever remember being mean to my father on purpose and he seemed to recognize what was happening. It made him angry in a way I had never seen before and I was surprised when my father didn't even try to hit me.

Instead, my father sent me out into the backyard and made me pull weeds until it was so dark I couldn't see what I was doing. I still don't understand why my father felt like that was a fitting punishment, but I felt a great sense of satisfaction as my hands got covered with grass stains and dirt.

38

★

That night, my mother came up to my bedroom and apologized for my father. Then she told me I shouldn't call him fat. My mother told me she didn't want me to make it any worse for myself than it already was. She told me it was easier to think of my father as heavy, but that just made him seem worse, even more overbearing, inescapable.

★

Sometimes, my father had to turn sideways to walk through doorways.

★

The first time my father beat me, I didn't understand what was happening to me. He palmed the side of my head like it was a ball and threw my head toward the living room floor. My body followed my head down to the rough carpet. I tried to get up, but I couldn't, and I didn't understand why I couldn't. I kept trying to get up, to stand up, to find some kind of balance, but my father kept pushing me down by my head and neck. It didn't hurt that much, but it was disorienting, the lack of control I had over my little boy body.

★

My father's hands seemed so huge to me then—and so fast. I could not get away from them.

★

Sometimes, I look at the hair on my arms and it makes me think of the hair on my father's scary arms.

★

Sometimes, my father would hold both of my wrists with his one hand while he slapped the side of my head with his other hand. I would try to get away from his slapping hand by moving sideways or ducking down. I would try to hide behind my own arms—try to keep my arms between us—but there wasn't too much else I could do. I was too little and too skinny to do much else besides bob or try to cover up.

★

If I ever cried when my father hit me, he would ask me if I wanted him to give me something to really cry about. I didn't, but I never answered him.

★

Sometimes, when I was angry with my father, I would go to this novelty shop that was in the mall and read the joke books, especially the ones with the *Yo mama's so fat* jokes, which I would convert to *Yo daddy's so fat* jokes as I read them. My plan was to memorize some of the fat jokes so I had comebacks for the times when I couldn't take how much my father was picking on me. Knowing the fat jokes was a strange kind of comfort, but I was always too afraid to actually say any of them to his face.

★

Yo daddy's so fat when he walks out of the grocery store wearing a red coat people yell, "Hey, Kool-Aid."

Yo daddy's so fat when he wears a yellow raincoat people yell, "Taxi!"

Yo daddy's so fat he takes a bath at the car wash.

★

Yo daddy's so fat he sweats mayonnaise.

Yo daddy's so fat his blood type is spaghetti sauce.

★

Yo daddy's so fat when he goes to the movies, he sits next to everybody.

Yo daddy's so fat he gets group discounts.

★

Yo daddy's so fat he shows up on radar.

Yo daddy's so fat he's got his own zip code.

★

Yo daddy's so fat when he died they had to take him out in two trips.

Yo daddy's so fat he wakes up in sections.

★

Yo daddy's so fat every time he turns around it's his birthday.

Yo daddy's so fat he sat on a dollar and it broke into four quarters.

★

Yo daddy's so fat when he walks his butt claps.
Yo daddy's so fat he broke a branch off the family tree.

★

I wouldn't have made fun of my father for being so fat if he hadn't been so mean. It felt good to be mean back.

★

Also, telling the jokes, even thinking the jokes, it still makes me feel better about my father. It is something beyond revenge.

★

When I think of my father, it is with a mixture of fear and disgust. When I try to look at him in my mind, it makes me look away.

★

I don't understand my complicated feelings about my father. I hated him, but I wanted him to like me. I was ashamed of him, but I wanted him to be proud of me.

★

Despite all the weight, my father was a good-looking man. People said so. It was the only thing that ever made me proud of him. My father took great care in how he looked. He always wore nice clothes and expensive cologne and different kinds of jewelry—big rings, thick bracelets, silver necklaces with cut-out coins for pendants. Also, he always combed his hair back in a certain way and he never went bald.

CHAPTER 10

I DON'T KNOW what caused my father's death, but there were a lot of things wrong with him. The most notable of my father's various ailments were high blood pressure, type-two diabetes, and the fact that he was obese.

★

The police officer who confirmed my father's death guessed that he probably died from a heart attack. The police officer said it didn't look like my father had struggled or been in a great amount of pain. He suggested my father's death happened quickly. There was supposed to be some kind of consolation in that.

★

Another possibility was that my father died from kidney failure, which might have resulted from the type-two diabetes and the high blood pressure. My father had a lot of symptoms associated with weak kidneys—including body swelling, confusion, fatigue, lethargy, and a kind of metallic taste in his mouth. My father's doctor had already talked with him about kidney dialysis and he probably would have started the treatment if he had lived much longer.

★

My father also had sores on the backs of his legs that wouldn't heal—in part because my father usually sat on the living room floor with his legs out in front of him—but that probably didn't kill him. It was probably just a symptom of poor circulation, which also caused his feet to swell so much that he often couldn't wear any of his shoes. Sometimes, my father's feet also got so dried out that the skin cracked and then got infected. Those sores didn't seem to heal either and my father's doctor warned him they would eventually have to amputate his feet if he didn't take care of them, but my father died before it ever came to that.

★

I'm glad my father didn't have a heart attack or a stroke, almost die, and then end up in the hospital for days or weeks. That would have been worse.

★

I wrote to the State of Michigan to request a copy of my father's death certificate. Weeks later, I received it in the mail and was oddly anxious opening the envelope. In the section for "Manner of death," somebody wrote, "Natural." In the section for "Chain of events that directly caused the death," somebody wrote, "Coronary atherosclerosis," which means his arteries were clogged with cholesterol, and then wrote, "Diabetes mellitus," which is just a more formal phrasing for diabetes. Below that, there is a section for "Other significant conditions contributing to death." There, somebody wrote, "Obesity, 500 lbs," with a plus/minus sign next to it, which meant it was a guess, more or less. They did not perform an autopsy on my father to determine any of this for certain.

★

I don't know if it counts as a kind of suicide—to eat yourself to death.

★

The death certificate notes that my father was pronounced dead on February 2, 2005, but it lists my father's date of death as January 28, 2005. There is something about that being noted in an official document that I find reassuring.

CHAPTER 11

AFTER HIGH SCHOOL, my father's parents made him leave the house. It may seem like a mean thing to do to an eighteen year old, but I understand why they didn't want him around.

★

At the time, my father didn't have a job or any place to live. He used to say he had three options—college, a job, or the armed forces. He didn't have the money or the grades to go to college and he didn't want to get up every morning to go to a job. About a month after high school, my father joined the Marines.

★

In the last photograph of my father before he joined the Marines, he's wearing a white T-shirt with the short sleeves rolled up. There is a cigarette tucked behind one of his ears and his arms are crossed over his chest. My father has a terrible smirk on his face and he looks like he feels pretty good about himself. Whatever he was doing right then, that could have been the high point of his life.

★

I have a rolled-up photograph that is four feet wide and has over two hundred Marines standing in it—their helmets on their heads, their rifles on their shoulders. I remember my father unrolling this photograph once when I was a little boy and pointing himself out. I remember how proud he seemed of this photograph from Camp Pendleton and it made me proud then to think of my father as somebody who fought in wars—an assumption I made and my father didn't correct.

★

I look at each face in that photograph, but I can't pick out the Marine who would become my father. I showed it to my mother and asked her if she knew which one he was, but she wasn't sure. It could have been a couple of different soldiers.

★

The first color photograph of my father is him in army fatigues. My father has his helmet on and his chinstrap snapped tight. There's a flag in the background. His face is freckled and there's a rifle in his right hand. It's the only time I have ever seen him look scared.

*

There's a black-and-white photograph of my father from when he was on leave from the Marines and came back home for Christmas. He's wearing his dress uniform and standing at attention in his family's living room. He is surrounded by flowered wallpaper and the angle of the photograph makes him look taller than the Christmas tree. It makes my father look like he's bigger than everything around him. I used to think of him that way when I was a little boy.

*

I remember looking at these photographs when I was a little boy and being fascinated by the idea of my father as a soldier. I imagined him defending our family and our house. I imagined him protecting us from Communist invasions. It made him seem taller and stronger than he ever could have been.

*

One fall, when I was maybe seven years old, my father went around the backyard shaking the lower limbs of the trees until their leaves fell to the ground. We raked them up and then took turns running and diving into the giant pile of leaves until the sun went down and it got cold. It was one of the few times I felt like my father and I understood each other.

*

Also, there was something about smashing through a pile of leaves so much bigger than me that made me feel like I could do anything. For that short time, I felt like I might grow up to be a giant.

*

I used to ask my father if he ever shot the enemy when he was in the Marines. He usually wouldn't answer, but sometimes he would explain to me that it was war and it wasn't like what happened on television. Then my father would get one of his rifles out of the closet and lay it into my open hands. He showed me how to hold the butt of the rifle against my shoulder and let me look through the scope as long as I didn't put my finger on the trigger.

*

For years, I would put on all green clothes and play soldier. I went on top secret missions in the backyard. I took cover in the bushes and the shrubs and in the tall weeds at the back of our lot. I protected the house from neighbors and trees and falling leaves. I protected the house from people walking by on the sidewalk and cars and trucks driving by on the street.

*

Once, I was playing soldier with my father's rifle in the living room. I had already sighted the lamp through the scope and then the television when I noticed my father had fallen asleep. I pointed the rifle at him and his face got huge. I centered the crosshairs between his eyes, but I didn't slip my finger off the guard and onto the trigger. Instead, I just mouthed, *Bang*.

★

After that, I started to imagine different ways my father might be killed. I imagined my father falling asleep while driving and dying in a car accident. I imagined him going through the windshield and being beheaded.

★

I imagined my father getting shot and killed in a hunting accident, then being left out there in the woods.

★

I imagined my father out fishing on a boat that was sinking and my father not being able to swim. I imagined my father thrashing in the water and then the water being still.

★

After reading about Gary Gilmore in the newspaper, I imagined my father getting shot and killed by a firing squad. I imagined each of the bullets hitting him and his body slumping against the wall.

★

At some point, my mother told me my father had never served in any war, had never been in any kind of combat, had never fired his rifle at anything besides a target. My mother told me my father had never shipped out, that the only fighting he ever engaged in was at home.

CHAPTER 12

WHEN MY MOTHER heard about my father's death, her first thought was that he probably killed himself. She had spoken with my father a few days before and he told her he wished he hadn't moved back to Michigan. My father said he should have stayed somewhere warm—either the Las Vegas he had recently left or somewhere in Southern California, where they had lived when they were a young couple.

I don't think my father meant much by that statement. He had said similar things to me many times, but my mother interpreted this to mean my father was lonely and depressed. She thought my father was suicidal and hoped he hadn't used one of his guns on himself.

★

I don't know why my mother thought it would be a messy death. It may have been because my father always left his underwear on the doorknob of the bathroom door every time he took a shower or because most of his ties had food stains on them. It may have been because she wanted to be angry with him about something. Also, it was their last conversation, so everything my father said during that telephone call took on more importance after he died than it had when she hung up the telephone.

★

During that last telephone call, my father also made a remark about getting one and a half kids in their divorce settlement. My father was trying to say he won my sister in the divorce. I was somehow split up between the two of them. The whole notion offended my mother, but my father never felt like he had enough of anything. He always wanted more of everything—money, food, shoes, clothing, magazines, hair, children, etc. Of course, I don't know why my father thought either of us kids were still his and I don't know why he thought we could be divided up as they had divided up the furniture and the money and the family heirlooms.

★

I don't remember my sister or me choosing sides.

★

I just realized my father thought both my sister and I should have sided with him after the divorce because my mother left him. That made her the bad parent instead of him.

*

During that last telephone call, my father also asked my mother if she would buy him a new house or a new car with the money she had inherited when her parents died. My father hated the fact that my mother's parents had died after my mother divorced him, which meant he didn't get any of that money. My father felt entitled to at least some of that inheritance after being married to my mother for over thirty-five years.

*

My father also knew my mother found it difficult to say no to him and he preyed on that feeling whenever he could. When my mother said no to buying him a new house so he didn't have to live in the little apartment he died in, my father asked her for a restored 1967 Corvette he had seen listed in the newspaper. My father was surprised when she agreed to buy it for him until she suggested that he would need to lose 200 pounds before he could get into the driver's seat. That's when my father hung up on my mother.

*

My mother hadn't liked my father for over ten years, so I don't know why she still talked to him after the divorce, except she still seemed to feel a certain responsibility for my father. She felt guilty for leaving him on his own. She knew better than anybody else that my father couldn't take care of himself.

*

Now that my father is dead, my mother wishes she hadn't been mean to him that last time they spoke, but it seems kind of fitting. As far as I know, that was the last time my father spoke to anybody.

★

My father's death was a kind of relief for all of us. We didn't have to watch him let himself die anymore.

CHAPTER 13

THERE AREN'T ANY standard wedding photographs of my parents. There isn't a photograph of them being pronounced man and wife. There isn't a photograph of the wedding party. There aren't any photographs of them cutting into the wedding cake or dancing the first dance as a married couple.

★

The only photograph from their wedding captures my mother and my father just before they are about to get into a car that has just married soaped on the rear window and strings of tin cans attached to the rear bumper. My father is wearing his Marine dress uniform and he's centered in the photograph. He's opening the passenger door for my mother as he turns back to look at the person taking the photograph. His smile is so wide and it's one of the few photographs that shows the gap between his front teeth. It makes him look as if he's about to do some damage.

My mother is in a strange position in the photograph. Her arms are out to her sides, the bouquet in one hand, and it looks like she's walking sideways. She looks caught by the camera's flash, which washes out the shiny blue fabric of her wedding dress.

★

Right after that photograph was taken, my parents started driving to California. It was their honeymoon, but only in the sense that moving to California was their honeymoon. My mother said it was sunny every single day for months after they moved there and it didn't seem like it would ever rain.

★

Here's how they met: My father was cruising in a car with his friends down the few blocks of a small town and my mother was walking down those same few blocks with her friends. My father yelled something and my mother yelled something back. That was it.

★

Because of how they met, my father always used to say my mother was a streetwalker when he met her. My mother would get embarrassed, but she wouldn't correct him.

★

Maybe it is because of how my parents met that the yelling between them went on for years. It became how they communicated with each other. Still, I have always wanted to know what those first words were. When I asked once, they both said they didn't remember, but then they looked at each other and smiled a little bit. I have always assumed they were too embarrassed to tell me or they thought I was too young to understand what the words really meant.

★

Once, after my parents had an argument about something I can't remember, I asked my mother what she liked about my father and she smiled. I hated that she seemed like a teenage girl when she told me about the way his hair was slicked back and how cute the gap between his front teeth was when he smiled. I hated that she liked the way his arms looked with the short sleeves of his white T-shirt rolled up. I hated that those things were what she told me.

★

The other thing my mother liked about my father was that her father didn't like him. My mother was supposed to be marrying up, but she fell in love down.

★

Another time, I asked my father what he liked about my mother and he got a different kind of smile on his face. My father told me my mother had long legs and was good at the hand jive.

59

I had no idea what either of those things meant until I was older. When I was a boy, every grown-up woman's legs looked long to me. It didn't seem like an important distinction. I just wish my father hadn't told me he fell in love with my mother because she gave him a hand job.

★

But my parents almost didn't get married. They almost never saw or heard from each other again. I almost wasn't conceived.

★

Here's what happened: After high school, my father went into the Marines and my mother went to college. My father lived in the barracks with dozens of other men and my mother moved into an apartment with a roommate who she didn't know particularly well. To fill in the space between them, my mother and my father wrote letters to each other for months.

Then, without any explanation, my mother stopped receiving my father's letters. Not long after that, my mother stopped writing letters to my father. Neither one of them knew what had happened. They both waited for months, thinking the other one had stopped writing.

★

What my mother didn't know was that my father was still writing her letters. What my father didn't know was that my mother wasn't receiving the letters. This was because my mother's roommate would come home to the apartment at lunch and steal my father's letters.

60

★

We only know this because one day my mother came home from work early and picked up the mail, which included a letter from my father. He was asking her why she hadn't written back. He was trying to understand what had happened between them.

★

My mother realized my father had been writing her all along and searched the apartment until she found the missing letters hidden at the back of her roommate's underwear drawer. My mother wrote my father back, explained what happened, and they started writing letters back and forth again. She moved out of that apartment and, a year later, when my father was back home on leave, my parents got married.

★

I don't remember what I was looking for in the attic when I found an old shoebox filled with the letters my father had written to my mother when he was stationed at Camp Pendleton. I don't remember any specifics from my father's letters, but I was fascinated by how much he wanted to be with my mother.

I was only twelve years old and I didn't quite understand my father's longing for my mother or how my mother could have been that desirable. I did not recognize the passionate soldier as my father or the beautiful girlfriend as my mother. I did not recognize the handwritten sentences as anything I had ever heard my father say out loud or as anything that would have ever been persuasive with my mother. I had never heard my father ask my mother for anything before. By the time I was old enough to understand what was happening between them, their relationship was mostly communicated in commands.

★

I could not reconcile the two people in the letters with what their marriage had become. After I read the letters, I looked at my parents in a different way. I realized they used to be different people.

★

That old shoebox didn't hold any of the letters my mother wrote to my father. He never saved them.

★

Years later, my mother found out her ex-roommate stole her next roommate's fiancé and married him. That made her feel lucky at the time.

★

A side note: After my mother stopped receiving my father's letters, she met a man named Carl in her astronomy class at college. He parted his hair on the side, wore button-down shirts, and looked like somebody who would get a good job someday. Within months, Carl and my mother were engaged. She was probably giving Carl hand jobs too.

★

A date was set and my mother and Carl started planning the wedding day. Somewhere in there, my mother found that letter from my father. The problem, my mother says, was that she loved both of them and didn't know how to choose. I don't know how my mother chose and she has never said, but she always seemed proud of the fact that two different men wanted to marry her.

My mother broke the engagement off with Carl by giving him back the engagement ring. The one my father gave her had a smaller diamond than Carl's. She described it as a diamond chip and sometimes she would hold it up in my father's face and try to make him feel small.

*

Sometimes, after my father said something mean to my mother, she would yell, "I should have married Carl."

In return, my father would yell, "I should have married a Tijuana whore."

*

Sometimes, growing up, we would see Carl in the grocery store with his family—a wife, a boy, and a girl—and I would wonder if he should have been my father.

CHAPTER 14

ANOTHER THING I think about with my father is him falling asleep on the couch in the living room, which happened nearly every night when I was growing up. The recurring image I have is my father watching the television and reading the newspaper at the same time—all spread out on the couch, his head tipped back, his mouth hanging open and snoring, a section of the newspaper opened up over his chest and stomach, the other sections of the newspaper scattered next to him on the cushions.

★

When I think about it, my father was asleep most of the time he was at home. I remember everybody else in the family trying to be really quiet whenever my father fell asleep in the living room. We spoke in whispers and tiptoed though rooms. It wasn't that any of us were afraid to disturb his sleep. It was more that my father couldn't do anything mean to us when he wasn't awake.

★

One of the reasons my father slept so much was sleep apnea, which he had because he was so fat. When a person is as fat as my father was, the extra soft tissue in the throat can block the airway and cause what is called a pause in breathing.

★

When I still lived at home, sometimes I sat in the living room and watched the sleep apnea happen to my father. I liked the part where his chest stopped moving up and down and he seemed to stop breathing. I liked the part where the lack of oxygen woke him up in a kind of shock and he choked and sputtered as he tried to breathe air back into his lungs. Sometimes, my father would look at one of us for some kind of explanation for what was happening to him and that always made him look helpless.

★

Sleep apnea would have put my father's body under a tremendous amount of stress, which would have contributed to his feelings of hunger and led him to eat even more food.

★

My father's episodes of sleep apnea happened dozens of times a night, so often that he got very little real sleep at night, which is why he often fell asleep during the day. Besides falling asleep while watching television and reading the newspaper, my father could fall asleep while he was eating dinner or talking on the telephone. My father could fall asleep while he was driving his pickup truck, which caused all kinds of accidents, but usually just little ones. His pickup truck was often at the repair shop for bodywork.

★

The only time my father visited my wife and me in our new house, he fell asleep on the toilet in the guest bathroom. It happened sometime during the middle of the night. The bathroom light was on and he was inside there when I got up in the morning. I went into the kitchen and started making breakfast, thinking we would eat together, but my father didn't come out of the bathroom.

I finished eating breakfast and waited a while longer. Eventually, I crept up to the bathroom door and listened for him. I was just hoping he wasn't dead.

★

When I got close enough to the bathroom door, I could hear him snoring softly. I was glad he wasn't dead.

★

I didn't knock on the bathroom door because I didn't want my father to realize I knew he had fallen asleep on the toilet. Instead, I used my cell phone to call the landline at our house and then I let the telephone ring until I had to leave a message.

I hung up my cell phone and listened. I heard my father moving around in the guest bathroom and then the toilet flushed and then he came out. My father walked into the kitchen and acted like he had just gotten up. My wife and I acted that way too. We were relieved he was alive.

★

My father may have died from complications associated with sleep apnea. My father may have suffocated himself with his fat and died in his sleep. Nobody ever tried to determine if that was, in fact, the case.

★

My father's sleep apnea, the snoring it caused was turbulent, violent, and full of animal sounds. The snoring was also part of why my mother divorced my father. She couldn't get any good sleep either. Plus, my father took up most of the bed. There was just enough room for my mother to lie there and not move.

CHAPTER 15

THE MORNING OF the first full day I was back in Michigan, I met my sister at my father's apartment so we could clean it out. Neither of us were sure what the state of my father's apartment would be or how much it would smell even though his body hadn't been inside there for a couple of days. We also weren't sure about my father's estate and whether he had made a will or not.

★

I arrived early and waited outside my father's apartment for my sister to get there with the keys. It was cold and I could see my own breath. It was quiet in a way that reminded me I was alone. I wanted to knock on the door to my father's apartment even though I knew there wasn't anybody inside.

★

The first thing I noticed when I walked into my father's apartment was the smell of death and shit. It made me turn my head even though the smell was cold, dried up, days old. That smell was mixed with my father's peculiar body odor, which was sharp and bitter but also had a faint sweetness to it.

★

That smell may have been caused by my father's adult-onset diabetes or it may have been caused by one of his other ailments. More obviously, my father's peculiar body odor might have been a direct result of how sweaty he often was, how much difficulty he had getting into the small shower in his apartment bathroom, and how much difficulty he had reaching and cleaning many parts of his body after he had become such a large man.

★

The second thing I noticed when I walked into my father's apartment was the stain he had left on the carpet in front of the couch. The carpet was a kind of beige apartment carpet and the stain was slightly darker than that. The carpet was plush, kind of dense and smooth. The stain was wide and loose, kind of lumpy and spread out.

★

I couldn't stop staring at the stain on the carpet. I couldn't stop thinking that my father had died right there. I couldn't stop thinking, That was him.

*

Eventually, my sister covered the stain up with a white sheet from one of my father's closets.

*

My mother showed up at my father's apartment later that afternoon. I told her she shouldn't have come over, that we didn't need the help, that it would be harder on her than it was on us. It seemed like the kind of thing an ex-wife shouldn't have to do for an ex-husband. But my mother hated the idea that my father might have left some kind of a mess for his children to clean up. My mother was still angry about the thirty-five years she had spent picking up after my father.

*

Once inside his apartment, my mother complained about my father's dirty laundry, the unmade bed, the dirty dishes left in the sink, and the fact that he hadn't taken the trash out. Of course, my father was dead and couldn't have taken the trash out for days. Also, my father probably didn't know he was going to die when he did.

*

At first, I didn't want to touch anything in my father's apartment. I stood there looking around the rooms at the way my father had lived and the things he was surrounded by when he died. There was a couch in the living room, an end table, and a recliner. There were a few things hanging on the walls—a collection of framed hat pins from some summer Olympics, a plaque he was given when he retired from the Accident Fund, and a print of San Clemente, where he lived with my mother after he was discharged from the Marines. There was an entertainment unit with a television in the center, a stereo system below that, and the surrounding shelves were filled with brand-name beer steins and Coca-Cola collectibles.

★

My father's apartment was filled with Coca-Cola collectibles—old glass bottles, a neon sign that didn't work, hat pins, and model cars. The clock on the living room wall was a Coca-Cola clock. My father ate off Coca-Cola plates and drank out of Coca-Cola glasses. I think the memorabilia reminded him of being a teenager in the 1950s—when everything seemed possible, before so much went wrong for him.

★

My sister bumped into me on purpose, nudged me, and shook me out of my stupor. I picked up a garbage bag and started throwing the obvious stuff away—old newspapers, junk mail, rotting food from inside the refrigerator, dishes that had started to grow mold.

★

My sister was going to take my father's recliner home and put it in her living room, but when we crouched down to pick it up— my cheek against the side of the recliner—the fabric felt sweaty and smelled bitter. We carried my father's recliner to the apartment complex's dumpster and then did the same thing with my father's couch. We threw away any of my father's furniture that was covered with any kind of fabric, as well as all the sheets and blankets. All of it smelled and was covered with a kind of human film.

★

The appliances in the kitchen had a different kind of film on them from all the greasy food my father cooked for himself. The frying pans were crusted with it and the many spatulas he left sitting out on the countertop—all of them had bits of dried up grease and food stuck to their edges.

★

Inside the bedroom, there was a new mattress, box spring, bed frame, and headboard. The mattress still had the plastic on it and I'm not sure he had ever slept on it. On top of the bed, there were two piles of clothes—one clean and one dirty. My father seemed to have used the bedroom mostly for storage and for getting dressed. There was a path to the closet and a path to a set of dresser drawers, but the rest of the bedroom was filled with exercise equipment my father didn't use—some dumbbells I found under a gigantic pair of sweatpants, a stationary bike I had put together for him and he never used, a treadmill with cardboard boxes sitting on its platform.

★

Another thing my father told my mother in their last telephone call: He said he was afraid to go to sleep. He was afraid he might not wake up. This must have been why my father didn't sleep in his bed in his bedroom.

★

My father had dozens of pairs of shoes in the bottom of his closet and all of them were stretched out from the spread of his feet as he got fatter and fatter, which might have helped keep him from tipping over. Also, the sides of some of his shoes were torn out or cut out to accommodate his foot width. Sometimes, my father wore sandals, even in the winter, because that was all he could get around his feet. I realized my father's clothes were too big for nearly anybody else to wear and all of them got stuffed into garbage bags and thrown into the dumpster.

★

One of my cousins took the television, the stereo, and the entertainment center. We gave the dining table and chairs to one of my father's neighbors in the apartment complex. We donated the bed, the exercise equipment, and anything else anybody else might want or use to Goodwill.

★

My sister and I mostly didn't want anything that had been my father's. In just a few hours, we had removed, thrown away, or given away nearly everything my father had accumulated during his lifetime.

★

My sister took my father's truck and used it as a trade-in to buy a new car, which has been undependable. She tried to sell the beer steins and the Coca-Cola collectibles online, but nobody else wanted the things our father collected.

★

There wasn't anything of my father's I really wanted, but there were some things I couldn't throw away. I had my father down to a cardboard box of things that included photo albums, his money clip, and a medical chain that said heart patient on it.

The photo albums were missing about half of their photos, which probably happened in the divorce. The money clip was an object of fascination for me when I was young enough to not understand how much money was worth. My father would pull that money clip out of his front pocket and there would be a big bill on the outside of all that folded up money and that always made me think he was rich. The medical chain—there is something reassuring about it. It reminds me that my father is dead.

★

There was another thing I took from my father's apartment, but only because it was mine: a coin collection I started when I was a boy. My father had his own coin collection and, at the time, I was young enough to want to do whatever my father did. I started looking at the date of every single coin that came into my possession, as well as any change my mother was given when she bought something. This went on for years. I had these slotted blue booklets to hold the coins and I pressed the coin for each year into a slot—Lincoln pennies and Indian Head pennies, Buffalo nickels and Jefferson nickels, Mercury dimes and then Roosevelt dimes, Washington quarters, Franklin half dollars and then Kennedy half dollars.

*

My father got me started, but we never really did it together. I don't know why I kept on collecting coins. I don't remember when I stopped checking the coins I received as change. But I do remember I left my coin collection on the top shelf of my closet when I went off to college. I couldn't find it when I moved all my belongings out of my parents' house years later. It was only after my father died and we were going through his possessions that I found it again. It was one of many things my father took from me and I got back.

*

There were a few things we didn't find after we had sorted through everything inside my father's apartment—a will, a handgun, and my father's wallet. We found a milk crate with folders of financial records, but most of the documents were old—canceled savings accounts, cashed out IRAs, an empty retirement account. There was a checking account with a few thousand dollars in it and a certificate of deposit worth a few thousand more.

My father would have still drawn social security if he hadn't died, but all the money from all his years of working jobs he hated was almost gone. My guess is he lost most of it gambling in Las Vegas, but I'm not sure, and he never would have admitted that anyway.

★

I knew to look for the handgun because my father showed it to me one of the last times I visited him. We were sitting in his living room and he pulled the handgun out of his pocket. He didn't say he just wanted to show me the gun.ji

He didn't say he wasn't going to shoot me. It was a little scary.

★

The pants my father wore were so wide and had such large pockets he could conceal a handgun in them. My father would never have admitted it, but I think he carried the handgun because he was afraid of getting mugged by somebody who noticed he didn't move well.

★

My father never shot anybody, but once his gun accidentally fired when he was cleaning it. My father said he didn't realize there was a bullet in the chamber.

*

When we were cleaning out my father's apartment, my sister found the bullet hole in the shared wall between his apartment and the woman who lived alone next door. I went over to ask the woman about it and she was happy to show me where the bullet had come through her side of the wall and then dented the freezer door on her refrigerator. That woman had even kept the slug, which she gave to me as a kind of souvenir.

*

It turns out the police had the handgun and the wallet. They were part of my father's belongings—the few things that were in his possession when he died—and they were returned to the family inside a sealed personal property bag after the police ruled my father's death wasn't a murder.

*

I don't know for certain, but I'm guessing that my father died while he was lying on his right side. The evidence for this is the fact that my father's wallet and his handgun—both of which he kept inside his right front pocket since he couldn't reach around to his back pockets anymore—were stained with and smelled like shit. It was what my father must have smelled like a couple of days after he died and that smell was captured in that sealed plastic bag.

*

One of the things I expected to find among the belongings the police returned was a silver coin that was probably a little bigger than a quarter. My father usually carried it with him, but it wasn't inside the sealed personal property bag with my father's loose change, his car keys, and his little tin of breath mints. The heads side of that silver coin was the top half of a naked woman from the front and the tails side was the bottom half of a naked woman from the back.

That silver coin was the first naked woman I ever saw and the outlined shape of her was amazing to me even though both sides of the coin had already been rubbed smooth in places from being handled so much. I was just a little boy then, but I looked at that silver coin so much I could close my eyes and turn those two incomplete images into one whole woman. Whenever I could, I would sneak into my parents' bedroom and look for that silver coin in the loose change and other things my father would leave up on top of his dresser when he changed into his home clothes after work. My father caught me doing this a bunch of different times, but he never punished me for it. He seemed to realize I wasn't trying to steal any of his money and I had become fascinated with what is underneath a woman's clothes.

★

The woman who ran the apartment complex asked us to pay my father's rent for the month of February. My father hadn't been alive for any of the days in February, but his body had occupied the apartment for the first few days of the month. The apartment manager explained that they were only asking because they couldn't rent the apartment to anybody else.

★

What the apartment manager didn't say was the stained carpet in the living room would need to be replaced and the bullet hole in the wall would need to be filled in and then the wall would need to be repainted. Also, it was going to be a while before my father's smell left the apartment. It was difficult to get away from my father whether he was alive or dead.

★

One of my father's things I didn't throw away was his address book, which is its own strange artifact. There aren't many names and numbers in it that haven't been crossed out. Some of the people probably died and some of them probably moved away. There must have been other people who my father stopped talking to and even more people who stopped talking to my father.

★

I called each of the telephone numbers that hadn't been crossed out and let those people know about my father's funeral. I didn't have to make many telephone calls, but some of them were difficult. There were a few people who needed to be reminded who my father was and I was surprised they had been able to forget him. I asked each of them how they did it, but none of them could explain.

CHAPTER 16

MY FATHER'S MILITARY career was not distinguished in any way, but his discharge during the summer of 1962 was honorable. Over the course of his two-plus years in the Marines, he rose from Private First Class (E-1) to Private First Class (E-2). This didn't seem like much, so I looked it up and found out that it was even less than I thought. The designation of (E-2) is an automatic advancement that takes place after six months of military service.

★

For the next two years after the Marines, my father worked on some kind of a press in a rubber mill. There is a photograph of him standing in front of his machine, which is taller and wider than he is. The machine had big metal tumblers that rolled out big sheets of rubber. My father is wearing these big safety glasses and gloves up to his elbows. He's scowling and his clothes are covered with black smudges.

★

I never heard my father mention this job. I only found out about it when I discovered an old résumé of his while I was cleaning out his apartment.

★

For the next three years after that, my father worked as a lab technician doing blood tests. He also started taking classes at the local community college—science classes, business classes, drafting classes, and a painting class. He could never train himself to type with more than one finger from each hand and flunked Typewriting I. He also flunked Principles of Accounting II and took an incomplete for his Topics in Management class.

My father took classes off and on for seventeen years at different community colleges. During this time, he earned a two-year degree in science and almost earned another two-year degree in business. My father was never too sure about what he was supposed to do.

★

In late 1966, my parents moved from California back to Michigan to be around family as they started their family. I was born early the next year on a Wednesday afternoon while my father was at work. He had a new job as a mechanical draftsman—drawing truck parts for a company called Diamond Reo—and he didn't want to leave work since he had been employed there for only a few months. I didn't know it then, but this was one of the first times my father wasn't there for me.

*

My mother liked to talk about how my father didn't drive her to the hospital. Supposedly, my father was at work, at lunch, eating a ham sandwich when he found out my mother's water had broken. That's why my mother was driven to the hospital by the next door neighbor, an old woman who often babysat me the first few years of my life and then died of lung cancer when I was four years old. The smoke residue from her chain smoking cigarettes was so thick I used to write my full name—Daniel Todd Carrier—on her living room walls with my finger.

*

Another thing about my birth: I was two weeks early and my father always blamed me for that. He made it seem like he wasn't ready for me. Growing up, he usually made me wait. Often, I wasn't allowed to sit down to dinner until he did.

*

For some reason, my father's parents, my grandparents, they always thought my name was Daniel Toad. I don't know if this was because of a misread version of a baby announcement or because of bad handwriting or because they couldn't spell very well. It could have been an elaborate joke my father and his parents were playing on me. Regardless, my father never corrected his parents and every year I received birthday cards addressed to Daniel Toad Carrier.

*

Once, my mother tried to explain to me that my Grandmother Carrier was kind of dumb, but I didn't understand how she could be that dumb. Those birthday cards only stopped after my Grandmother Carrier died of a heart attack in a trailer park outside Las Vegas. I didn't want to be glad she was dead, but it felt right.

★

Sometimes, when I was little, my father used to call me Tiger and that always made me feel really good.

CHAPTER 17

ON ONE OF the kitchen counters in my father's apartment, he lined up twenty-four different bottles of prescription medication. Most of the prescriptions were to treat his diabetes, but there were also two prescriptions to treat high blood pressure, one for high cholesterol, one for excessive water retention, and one prescription was an arthritis medication that was later taken off the market when it was found to cause heart attacks. So my father might have been killed by his arthritis medication or it could have been the diabetes medications, one of which has since been linked to strokes and to heart attacks.

*

I don't know if my father was actually taking all twenty-four of those medications. He used to talk about his doctor changing one medication for another because of one side effect or another, but there were so many prescriptions and symptoms and side effects that it was too difficult to keep track of them.

*

My father used old breath mint tins to keep track of his pills, one tin for each day of pills. When I found the breath mint tins on his kitchen counter, every one of them was empty. It's possible my father stopped taking his medication and that is what killed him.

*

I don't know whether all my father's medications kept him alive or whether some of them killed him. I do know the prescriptions only kept him alive for just so long.

*

I want to know how many days of his life all those pills were worth.

CHAPTER 18

MY PARENTS DIDN'T have very much money the first few years after they moved back to Michigan. I don't remember that time, of course, but apparently we lived in a series of rental houses that were identified by their particular infestations. We lived in the mouse house, the spider house, the raccoon house, and the cockroach house. My father remembered turning the lights on before entering any room. My mother remembers leaning over my crib and wiping bugs off my forehead.

★

Once, my parents couldn't get me to stop crying. They couldn't figure out what was wrong with me. My mother says my father talked her into ignoring me. He said I would stop crying if they stopped picking me up and trying to comfort me.

★

After a few days, my mother took me to the doctor, who thought I might have an ear infection. I didn't, but I did have a spider living inside my right ear.

★

There's a photograph of my father and me lying in my parents' bed. I'm about two years old and I'm lying where my mother usually was in their bed. The sheet is pulled up over our stomachs and our hands are on top of it. My father and I are turned toward each other and smiling at each other. I'm trying to remember what that must have felt like.

★

Not long after that photograph was taken, my sister was born. My father didn't make it to the hospital for her birth either. He was deer hunting with his younger brother somewhere in the woods of Northern Michigan. The same day my father brought home the carcass of a six-point buck, my mother brought home my week-old sister.

★

I don't know who took care of me during that time when I was two years old and neither one of my parents was at home. I don't think I was left at home on my own.

★

Not long after that, there's a photograph of my father sitting on the couch. He's holding my sister in his arms and has his face turned down toward hers. I'm sitting at the other end of the couch in nearly the same posture—my arms folded across my chest, my face turned away, looking at something outside the frame. I wasn't old enough to understand what was happening in the family, but I already seemed to know that my sister was the favorite.

★

There's a photograph of me opening presents on Christmas morning, 1970. I'm smiling and holding up a new pair of black cowboy boots. I'm so happy that I'm holding the cowboy boots out to the camera.

My father is behind me in the photograph, sitting off to the right. He is staring back at me with a blank look on his face. Either he is really tired or he doesn't care.

★

I wonder if my father didn't like it when I was happy.

★

There's a photo of me from when I'm about four years old. My mouth is dropped open and I'm looking at my father with a facial expression that's some mixture of surprise, hurt, bafflement, and disappointment. It may have been my father's version of teasing me—which could be brutal or devastating but never fun or funny—but I don't know what exactly my father had just done to me that particular time or why my mother felt the need to capture it with a photograph.

89

★

My father is still thin in all those photographs, but I don't ever remember him looking like that. When I see him thin, I think it's a different person. I feel like I had a different father than the one in those photographs.

★

I went through a stage where I would walk into whatever room my father was in and turn the lights off. I never told anybody why, but I was trying to make him disappear.

★

My father would call out when he came home from work and, when I was a little boy, this was an exciting time in the house. For a time, my sister and I would run to the front door and hug his leg or jump up and down around him. My father standing just inside the front door having just come home from work, that was one of my happiest memories for a time.

★

It was around this time I noticed my mother wasn't as happy about my father's daily homecoming as my sister and I were. Often, she wouldn't hug him or go to the front door or even say anything to him. If my mother didn't greet my father in any way, which happened enough for me to notice it, then he would wait until my sister and I let go of him and say something mean to my mother. Then it would get really quiet. I remember looking back and forth between my mother and my father until it felt scary.

★

Here's one of the insults I remember: "Your mother seems to be lost in thought. It's someplace she's never been before."

My father would laugh and get my sister and me to laugh with him. It was confusing that things could be funny and mean at the same time.

★

My mother and my father were really good at being mean to each other. Sometimes, when my father stood up, my mother would look at him and say, "I always wanted a taller husband."

My father wasn't a short man, but this was one of my mother's standard insults—in part, because Carl was a tall man. Plus, there wasn't anything my father could do to change how tall he was.

★

The thing I remember most about the taller insult was how it filled me with a strange feeling of power. I was just a little boy and I was going to grow bigger and get taller. I made a pact with myself to grow up to be taller than my father. It felt like something I could control.

★

My father used to find different ways to insult my mother. He would say things like, "You wouldn't be so ugly if you were a redhead." Or, "Are you always this stupid, or is today a special occasion?"

★

At the time, I didn't understand these insults. I could see how much he liked her when he looked at her.

★

Sometimes, when my father came home, my mother would say, "I was hoping you were somebody else." She would usually say it with a really pretty voice, which made it confusing, but pretty soon my mother and my father would start arguing, and that would turn into the kind of yelling that was too loud and too fast to follow.

★

Sometimes, I think that was how I learned to talk—loud and fast. I don't know why none of the other adults I was around ever corrected me. It was my kindergarten teacher, Mrs. Fisher, who taught me how to use my quiet voice.

★

In my family, it was usually the last person talking who won the argument, but my father could also win any argument by raising his hand back over his head. The only consolation was that his hand was usually open-palmed and not a fist.

★

I tried it on my mother once, but it didn't work. She sent me to my room.

★

Once, my parents had an argument because my mother set out slices of bread with dinner instead of dinner rolls. My father knocked over his chair when he stood up from the dinner table. He made the whole house shake when he slammed the back door on his way out of the house.

★

For my father, good bread was an important distinction between the poor farm family he grew up in and the middle-class family he expected us to be. That is why we had family dinners on Sundays. That is why we ate so many pot roasts.

★

My father could fight about anything—bread, haircuts, light bulbs, newspapers, cats, boots, chicken, belts, pickles, chairs, lottery tickets, playing cards, potato chips, cheese and crackers, socks, after-shave, dishes, combs, loose change—anything.

★

When I was a boy, long before I had four knee surgeries, I used to love to run. Every weekday evening around 5:30, I waited at the end of the block for my father's pickup truck to turn the corner onto our street and then raced him to the driveway of our home.

I used to think, Can't he see how fast I am?

★

I used to be a boy with a father.

★

During the mid-1970s, there was a gas crisis. People stopped buying as many cars and trucks and companies like Diamond Reo had to lay off workers, including my father. A lot of fathers in our neighborhood lost their jobs then and the summer of 1975 was strange with so many of them at home so much of the time. Most of us had never had our fathers pay so much attention to us and we didn't quite know what to do.

We still played baseball and basketball and rode our bikes up and down the street, but one father would come out to throw us some pitches or shoot jumpers and then another father would and pretty soon it would turn into these brutal father-son contests that didn't end until somebody got hurt.

★

In the fall of 1975, my father started working as a safety inspector for a company called the Accident Fund. There was all kinds of gear that came with his new job—plastic helmets with face shields, eye goggles with a thick rubber strap, long rubber gloves, and different colored ear plugs. I had no idea what my father did with those things when he went to that job. I didn't understand how somebody could inspect safety. It seemed more likely that my father somehow caused accidents, but I didn't understand how that could be a job somebody would get paid for. Sometimes, when my father left the gear around the house, I would run around with it on. It made me feel like a person from the future.

★

Years later, I learned my father's job was to make companies install safety protocols to keep people from getting hurt at work. I don't want to talk about how ironic that is, but what if he would have done that at home too?

★

I remember the few times my father and I played catch. I can still see the baseball in the air between us.

★

Also, I always liked it when he came home from work and I was playing basketball in the driveway. I would pass my father the basketball and he would shoot a two-handed set shot before going into the house. He almost always missed and I would chase after the ball.

★

One Saturday afternoon, my father took me to a shooting range. After a gun safety class, I got to shoot his rifle, a .30-30 Winchester. I remember two things about that time: (1) I missed the target by so much we had no idea where the bullet went. (2) The kickback from the rifle made my shoulder hurt for days. I still don't know what my father was trying to teach me that afternoon.

★

One of the other things I remember doing with my father is playing cards—gin rummy, cribbage, euchre, war—any game that could be won or lost. He taught me to play cards, in part, because my mother didn't like cards and wouldn't play with him. I was just the next available body, but it still made me feel special. It felt like he had chosen me.

★

I was ten years old when my father taught me how to play poker. That first time, he told me to go get my piggy bank and he'd teach me a new game. We emptied my piggy bank and split up my life savings. I didn't understand why we were only playing with my money—especially since I knew there was a pile of change on top of his dresser—but I still wanted to play.

The game was five card draw and I understood which hands were better than other hands, but I didn't understand when to bet, raise, or fold at the right times. That afternoon, I lost all my money to my father and developed a great need to beat him. I learned how much I liked gambling and how much I didn't like my father.

★

I wanted to play poker again, but my father didn't give me any of my money back. He left all my change on his side of the kitchen table and I knew I couldn't take any of it back even though he had used half of my life savings to win the other half of my life savings from me. I put my empty piggy bank back in my bedroom and thought about how I would play my hands the next time.

★

Over time, my father taught me how to play five card draw, five card stud, seven card stud, Texas hold'em, Omaha, Omaha high-low, lowball, and other variations on poker. We never used wild cards. My father didn't like the way they changed the odds.

★

Once, for his birthday, I bought my father scratch-off lottery tickets. After he scratched all of them off—and didn't win anything—he told me I bought the wrong ones.

★

One of the grossest memories I have of my father is him making breakfast. He would stand over a frying pan wearing nothing but tight, stretchy, red bikini briefs. His underwear was always too small for him, so the crack of his butt stuck out above the waistband and his stomach fat hung down over the front.

The grease would spit and pop in the frying pan. He would stick one hand in his underwear and scratch himself in a way that couldn't be ignored while he worked the spatula with his other hand. He liked his eggs greasy and over easy. He fried his bacon until it was burnt.

★

When I was a little boy, my disgust mechanism would kick in and I wouldn't be able to finish my breakfast. I would get in trouble for that, but I would get up and leave the kitchen anyway. Even today, the smell of greasy eggs still makes me feel queasy.

*

After my father died, I was remembering the underwear and the eggs with my sister and she was dumbfounded. The smell of greasy eggs makes her sick too. Her therapist wonders if that smell is a trigger for something that happened to us, but neither one of us can remember what happened after we left the kitchen.

*

My father's life was an ordinary one in so many ways. I wonder if I am making him into something more than he was because he was my father.

*

At the back of my father's sock drawer, under some dress socks he never seemed to wear, there was a black-and-white photograph with scalloped edges that had curled up over the years. The photograph was a close-up, two sets of fingers pulling apart something hairy and fleshy and slick. I found the photograph when I was six years old. I didn't realize what it was until years after that.

*

There is about a seven-year gap when there aren't any photographs of my father. During this time, he grows sideburns and gets fat. The next time we see my father, he is standing on the patio behind our house wearing a black tank top and grilling hamburgers. His face is glistening with sweat in nearly the same way the hamburgers are glistening with fat on the grill. This is the father I remember, Big Ray.

★

My father loved to barbecue and it didn't even have to be summer for him to go out on the patio and light up the grill. He would even stand out there during the winter—in his shirtsleeves, no coat—turning over the hamburger patties and strip steaks with a pair of tongs until the meat was burnt on both sides. He didn't like even a hint of blood in his cooked meat. The fire colored his face mean.

★

Sometimes, in the mornings before school, my father would look at the way I was dressed and say, "Looking sharp." That always made me feel really good.

★

There's a photograph of my father sitting at a picnic table and holding up an empty plate. He looks pretty happy in that shot.

★

Once, my mother and sister and I were all sitting at a picnic table—with the summer food all lined up in the middle—and we were waiting for my father before we started eating. He sat down on one end and the whole picnic table tipped—the food all sliding toward him and onto the ground before he could stand back up. What I'm trying to say is this: All three of us together wasn't enough against my father.

★

My father broke furniture. There were certain chairs my father did not sit on. Every couch that was ever in our house eventually had a small stack of bricks under the frame where it had cracked so people could still sit on it without sliding into the middle. My parents' bed had two-by-fours laid across the bed frame to support the cracked box springs and keep the mattress from sagging into the middle too.

★

Sometimes, I feel like my father is sitting in the chair next to my desk. He's a ghost now and thinner. I'm not worried about him breaking the chair.

★

My mother took my sister and me to church every Sunday morning, but my father never went with us. He always stayed home in bed with the newspaper and I couldn't figure out why my father wasn't worried about going to hell. How could he not be afraid of Our Heavenly Father?

Eventually, I asked him if he believed in God and his answer was halting and awkward. His botched response was the first thing to make me wonder if God actually existed and I realized I might not have to be afraid of God either.

★

It took me longer to realize I didn't have to be afraid of my father.

★

My father used to do this thing when we were in public and he didn't want to be seen yelling at me or hitting me. He would put his arm around me and rest his hand on my shoulder in a way that must have looked affectionate to anybody who saw it. Then he would grip some muscle in my shoulder so hard that it would make me seize up. The gesture must have made him look like a good father, but I wouldn't be able to move or talk or even scream out in pain.

★

I will still startle if somebody puts an arm around my shoulder that way.

★

Once, after my father had knocked me down over something, I got back up, ran at him, and launched my whole body toward his midsection. I was trying to ram him or tackle him, something like that, do as much damage as I could. I felt like this action was somehow going to change things between us, but I just bounced off my father and fell back down, my arms open and empty. He didn't move, except to lift one of his feet and kind of nudge my shoulder with it.

★

Another time, I left a drinking glass on an end table and my father told me to pick it up and take it into the kitchen. For some reason I don't remember and can't explain, I refused to do it. My father hit me and told me again to pick it up. I refused again and he hit me again. I remember standing there, not moving and not saying anything as he hit me over and over again. Right then, I didn't feel like there was anything my father could do to really hurt me. I felt like I could absorb so much pain and still walk away from it.

★

One of the things I found in my father's papers was the program from his twenty-fifth high school reunion. There is a little biography for everybody in the class of 1957 and my father's says he worked in engineering at Diamond Reo—even though he worked as a draftsman. It also says he was working as a safety engineer—even though he was a safety inspector. My father wasn't what he wanted to be. My father wasn't what I wanted him to be either.

★

After my first girlfriend broke up with me, my father told me I would have lots of girlfriends even though I was pretty sure then I would never have another girlfriend. After he said that, he handed me an old copy of *Playboy* magazine from his stack on the top shelf of the closet. He said, "Pictures of naked girls aren't as much trouble as real girls."

★

That was supposed to be some kind of advice and it was one of two times my father gave me any kind of advice. The other time was after I came home from a date with Ellen Bonner. He was drunk and said, "I recommend the blow job. Nobody ever got pregnant from a blow job."

★

My father hated it when I talked on the telephone to Ellen Bonner, especially when it was a school night. We only had one telephone and if anybody talked on it for more than a couple of minutes, my father would start screaming about the line needing to be open. He thought somebody else might be trying to call the house even though nearly everybody knew they weren't supposed to call our house after dark. For a while, I did as he said, but, eventually, I wanted to talk to Ellen Bonner more than I feared what my father might do to me if I didn't get off the telephone.

★

Sometimes, my mother would stand in the kitchen next to the telephone and kind of guard it from my father, but there wasn't much she could do to save me from him. I had never really defied my father before, but I would turn away from him as he screamed at me. I would hold the telephone tight to one ear and the palm of my hand over my other ear. I could still hear my father yelling at me and Ellen Bonner could hear him yelling through the telephone, but we would keep talking like it wasn't happening.

★

At some point, I started stretching the telephone cord across the kitchen and talking to Ellen Bonner outside on the patio. It helped having the sliding glass doors between my father and me. I could still see him and hear him, but the glass between us made it seem as if it wasn't real—as if it was something I was watching happen on the television or a movie screen.

★

I knew I was usually going to get a beating when I came back inside the kitchen and hung up the telephone, but that only happened when my father was still awake. Sometimes, I would stay on the line with Ellen Bonner as long as I could just to postpone the beating. Sometimes, she would have to hang up, but I would keep talking and listening as if she was still on the other end of the line. Other times, my father would fall asleep on the couch in the living room and I could sneak up to my bedroom without getting any kind of beat down.

★

I don't know why my father waited for me to hang up the telephone instead of just holding down the cradle so we were disconnected. All I can think of is that my defiance gave him an excuse to beat me, which he seemed to want to do and which somehow seemed acceptable to me at the time.

★

Eventually, I started to fight back even though I wasn't big enough or strong enough to do any real physical damage to my father. I was still just a skinny teenage boy and my father was a full-grown man. Plus, my father weighed double what I did then and he also had really fast hands. It usually didn't last too long and he usually didn't leave marks on me. There were almost never any cuts or bruises on my face or on the lower parts of my arms, nothing that could be seen above my collar or below my short sleeves.

★

Sometimes, I landed a punch on his arms or in his stomach, but I'm not sure he ever felt those. One time, I knocked the wind out of him when I kicked him in the chest as I was running up the stairs trying to get away from him. Another time, I caught him with an elbow in the neck. It was really satisfying to hear him gasp for breath and see him hold his neck with both of his hands as if he was choking himself.

★

The beatings didn't stop until after the time my father fell backward down the stairs and hit the back of his head on the landing. He looked crumpled at the bottom of the stairs and he always stood with a little hunch after that. I felt a little stronger and a little taller than I had just before that happened.

★

Sometimes, I still get the urge to fight my father. If my father weren't dead, I would kick his ass.

*

My relationship with my father shifted after the beatings stopped. I was eighteen years old and I started calling him Big Ray. For some reason I can't explain, my father seemed to think me calling him the nickname made him cool.

*

Another thing: I stopped bringing any of my girlfriends around the house because of the way my father looked at each of them—always staring at different body parts, but not really looking at their faces. I watched him stare at Melanie Durbin as she sat down and then as she stood up—always trying to get a glimpse up a skirt or down a top. He saw me catch him, but he didn't stop, and I became afraid for her too.

*

When I was a teenager, I learned how to leave a room whenever my father entered it. The timing of this was important. It had to be done while he was still sitting down or getting settled. We got along much better that way.

*

In 1985, my parents celebrated their twenty-fifth wedding anniversary. My mother's maid of honor threw a big party and I didn't understand how everybody was so happy for them.

In front of everybody, my father gave my mother a huge emerald ring, which seemed to confuse her. She seemed to be wondering if he might actually love her in a way she had forgotten. But the emerald ring was just an extravagant gesture, a kind of performance my father was so good at outside the house, the loving husband and the good father.

★

After I graduated from high school, I moved out of the house and hours away for college. I only saw my father on certain holidays, a couple of winter breaks and spring breaks, and one summer when I couldn't find a job at college. I don't know as much about my father after I got away. I felt terrible about leaving my sister behind.

★

Sometimes, I try to figure out how different I might have been if my father had been nicer to me. Would I try as hard as I do? Would I be happier than I am? Would I have a different wife? Would I have children instead of cats? Would I be a schoolteacher instead of a writer? Would I ever have moved away from home? Would I be more sad, but less torn up?

★

After college, I moved even farther away from home and stopped going home for holidays. I stopped calling home too. I became so busy with my own life that I began to forget my father.

107

CHAPTER 19

I DON'T REMEMBER the name of the funeral home that took care of my father's dead body, but it had a somber name. I don't remember the name of the funeral director either, but I do remember sitting across the desk from him as he told my sister and me what the options were—burial or cremation, casket or urn, open or closed. There could be a funeral with the body or a memorial service without the body.

★

The funeral director suggested we might not want an open casket and then wrinkled up his face. It was his gentle way of letting us know our father's body had decomposed during the five days before anybody realized he was dead. The funeral director also let us know our father would require what was known as a Goliath casket and that would cost extra, if we decided we did want to bury him in a casket.

★

As far as we knew, our father didn't make any arrangements for himself. We didn't know how he wanted his death to be handled. We didn't even know if he wished to be buried or, if he did, if he wished to be buried in a particular cemetery or in a particular city—Lansing or Las Vegas or even San Clemente.

We didn't know if he wished to be cremated or, if he did, if he wished for his ashes to be kept in an urn or scattered in some particular place in the world—a river or a lake he used to fish in, one of the casinos where he used to play poker, or maybe one of the drive-in restaurants that served draft root beer and his favorite Coney Dog.

★

One of the awkward parts of deciding what to do with my dead father was when my living mother offered one of the cemetery plots she had inherited from her parents. This meant my father would have been buried with my mother's family and my father would have hated that. Also, it seemed wrong, the idea of their two dead bodies being buried next to each other forever after they had divorced.

★

We decided on a memorial service instead of a funeral service. My father would not have wanted a minister to say anything about his life. My father would not have wanted anybody to say anything about his life. I understand the implications of that. I didn't always do what my father wanted me to do.

★

We decided to have our father cremated. It avoided the question of an open or a closed casket. It also avoided the posthumous embarrassment of the Goliath casket. These were quiet ways we honored our father.

★

I paid for as much of the final arrangements as I could with the money from my dead father's wallet. I put the rest of it on a credit card.

★

Having a dead father is distracting. Sometimes, in the months after he died, I forgot where I was driving a car or what I was doing in a particular room. Sometimes, I would find myself just standing in the middle of the kitchen or looking at myself in the mirror over the bathroom sink.

★

I wanted to think the death of my father wasn't affecting me, but I forgot to pack any nice clothes to wear at my father's memorial service. I didn't bring a jacket or a tie or even a belt. That's how I realized I wasn't being myself.

★

Whenever I am thinking about my father being dead, I feel like I am being somebody else. Whenever I am not thinking about my father being dead, I feel like I am being myself.

★

Generally, a funeral service or a memorial service is supposed to take place within several days of the person's death, but my father had probably been dead for five days before anybody found him, so the memorial service was three days after that.

★

A lot of people sent flowers. Most of the people who came to the memorial service were family, but there were also a lot of old neighbors, a few people he went to high school with, and the guys he played poker with. I know some of these people attended the memorial service out of a sense of obligation, but it was more people than I expected, and I wanted to think a good number of the people cared about my father. It made the end of his life seem a little less lonely than it probably was.

★

Toward the end of the visiting hours, a woman who nobody seemed to know walked into the memorial service. She looked at me and said, "You must be his son." She said, "He left his mark on you."

I disliked her as soon as she said it, but I kept talking with her. I didn't want to be anything like my father and I wanted to know who she was. She turned out to be a nurse who worked with my father's doctor. She said my father always talked about his kids and he always made her laugh. I was surprised to find out my father talked about my sister and me with strangers. I didn't feel like we were talking about the same person.

★

I am the only person who traveled a great distance to be at my father's memorial service.

★

I still don't like my father, but I still miss him.

★

My father's best friend for most of his life was Stanley Rogan. They went through school together, joined the Marines together, and stayed friends with each other even as each of their wives left them. At the memorial service, I asked Stanley to tell me a story about my father and he told me about a night of drinking in San Clemente, California, in 1960.

My father and Stanley had been out at a bar near the beach, then gotten into some kind of skirmish with some surfer guys. The police showed up and Stanley remembers my father and him running out the back of the bar, through backyards and alleyways, and then hiding in somebody's sailboat until they were sure nobody was chasing them anymore. Stanley said, "It felt like a chase scene in a movie."

They snuck back to the apartment my father shared with my mother and, by the end of the night, they were crushing empty beer bottles in the garbage disposal (a relatively new appliance at the time) and playing the radio as loud as it would go. Eventually, the garbage disposal jammed and the radio stopped playing. After that, my father unplugged the radio and started swinging it by the cord around and around over his head. Then my father let the radio fly across the living room and yelled, "Play, damn it," as it crashed into the walls of the apartment. He repeated this until the radio was broken into pieces and they were out of beer.

★

I don't feel like that guy was my father.

★

After my father died, I found it difficult to accept any kind of sympathy from anybody. People called on the telephone to offer their condolences. They sent flowers and cards and I did not want any of it. All I could think was this: It's better that he's dead. I resented the idea that my life might be better if my father was alive.

CHAPTER 20

ONCE, AS A baby, I was sick and the family doctor called in a prescription to the local pharmacy. My father was supposed to pick it up on the way home from work, but he didn't come home until late, and he didn't have the prescription with him when he did. My mother was angry about the forgotten medicine, but also because he was drunk and because it had become obvious he was having an affair.

My mother says my father got angry at her for being angry with him and he started choking her. My mother remembers him pressing his thumbs on her windpipe and almost passing out. She remembers thinking it seemed like a stupid way to die.

My mother says she stopped fighting him and went limp and my father stopped choking her. He let go of her neck and she dropped to the floor. She remembers hitting her head on the hardwood floor, which made a dull sound loud enough to make me start crying, which made her jump up to go to me, but my father already had me in his arms. My mother says she wanted to take me away from him, but was afraid of what might happen if she tried.

*

I was too young to remember anything about that time when my father choked my mother and she didn't tell me about it until after he was dead. But sometimes my father would ask my mother if she remembered when he almost choked her to death and then my mother would ask my father if he ever worried about his dinner being poisoned. And then they would both start laughing. My sister and I always thought it was a joke.

*

My mother once told me she dominated their relationship for the early years they were together. She said she doesn't remember when that changed.

*

When my mother walked past my father, he would slap her on the butt really hard—so you could hear it, so even the sound was a little scary—or he would grab her by one of her arms and pull her down until she fell into him. Then he would hold on to her while she struggled to push herself away from him and stand up again. When I was a boy, I thought this was just a rough kind of affection that probably happened in most homes and families.

*

I don't remember my father ever choking me, but he would do this thing he called a *bear hug*, which was so hard and so slow I wouldn't be able to breathe again until the bear hug was over. I have been afraid of bears ever since.

★

I'm not really afraid of bears.

★

As I got older and stronger, I began to struggle against my father's bear hugs. I was still mostly helpless, but sometimes I could get an arm loose and try to push myself away from his body. This became what my father called *wrestling* and, eventually, I learned to use my legs for some kind of leverage. I learned my father would let me go if I got a little bit of a kick in. Years after my father died, my mother and I somehow started talking about this. She was surprised when I told her I never liked it. She thought we were playing.

★

I just remembered something else: When we would *wrestle*, my father would pin me down and rub his scratchy sideburns against my cheek or neck or any other exposed skin. It was unbearable in a visceral way and part of the reason I hated the smell of my father and part of the reason I have never worn cologne and part of the reason my wife never wears perfume.

★

I don't remember my father ever hugging me nice when I was growing up. I don't remember my father ever kissing me goodnight. I don't know if he did any of that when I was little, before I could really remember those kinds of things.

★

I do remember how I usually had to go to bed before my father came home at night. This was when I was five or six or seven years old and I still liked my father. Those nights, my mother would tuck me into bed and kiss me on the forehead. Then I would ask my mother to ask my father to come upstairs to my bedroom and kiss me goodnight when he got home.

I used to have terrible nightmares and the thought of my father coming up to my bedroom to kiss me goodnight, to exhibit some sign of human affection, was comforting to me then. I usually couldn't sleep as I listened for my father to come home, but I always fell asleep before he did.

★

I don't think my father ever came up to my bedroom and kissed me goodnight. I think I would have woken up. I think I would have recognized him as a monster.

★

I don't remember this, but, apparently, my sister would throw a temper tantrum about going to bed unless my mother promised her my father would come in and kiss her goodnight when he came home from night school. My mother says my father would go into my sister's bedroom and lie down in her bed with her. My mother says she peeked in sometimes, but there was only a night-light in my sister's bedroom, and she couldn't really see anything.

★

My sister says she doesn't remember my father coming into her bedroom and kissing her goodnight, but my mother had been thinking about it again after my father died. My mother says she had suspicions and hopes my father didn't do anything terrible to my sister. The way she said it made me think she knew he had.

★

Growing up, my father was always asking my sister to give him a kiss and my sister always did. It always made me feel uncomfortable for some reason I didn't understand when I was a little boy. I didn't think it was because my father never asked me to give him kisses. I knew I didn't want to do that with him.

★

There's a photograph of my father with my sister. He is holding her against him with one arm and she is smiling and laughing as she presses into him and kisses him on the cheek. This could be a really sweet and innocent moment between a father and a daughter. But at the edge of the photograph, my father's other hand isn't holding her in the same way. His other hand is cupping the cheek of her butt.

★

My father asking my sister to give him kisses, that lasted until she was a teenager. One night, after she came home from the first date she ever had with a boy, my father called her a whore. My sister and the boy had gone to the movies and then gotten ice cream cones.

CHAPTER 21

MY FATHER BECAME a grandfather when my sister gave birth to a baby boy in 1988. There is a photograph of my father holding his first grandchild out in front of him, at arm's length, trying to give him away. Being a grandfather did not change my father in any way I remember or recognized.

★

There is another photograph of my father where he's sitting at the dining table with both of his grandchildren, a boy and a girl—one on each leg, one arm around the waist of each of them. There are plates and bowls and platters of food between them and the camera. All three of them are laughing and I'm guessing that my sister must have said something funny. She could always get my father to laugh when she wanted to.

★

I don't know who is taking the photograph, but it is a holiday shot from 1993. The Christmas tree and my father take up most of the shot. My mother is there too, but she is mostly cut off. It's just her one arm and shoulder, her one leg and hip.

★

Not long after that, my mother separated from my father. She didn't tell anybody she was leaving him or where she was living. My father said he came home from work one day and my mother wasn't home. Then he noticed the bed from the guest room was gone, her closet was empty, and the family photos were missing from the walls. My father said dark rectangles of dust surrounded the spaces where the photographs had been hanging on the walls. He said the house was filled with other missing things.

★

One of the few things my mother ever said about this period in her life is this: She was afraid of what might happen to her if my father found her. I was proud of my mother for doing something she was afraid to do.

★

Once, my father told me he tried to find my mother after she moved out of their house. Nobody knew where my mother was living but her. My father drove his pickup truck up and down the side streets of Lansing, East Lansing, and the surrounding communities looking for her car. He looked for her car in the driveways and in the garages of people she knew. Sometimes, if nobody was home, he would look in the windows of their houses for anything that might have been hers.

★

My father thought my mother had rented an apartment after she moved out, so he mostly drove through the parking lots of apartment complexes looking for her car. Sometimes, he parked in empty parking spots, ate bags of fast food, and waited for apartment buildings to fill up with people.

★

Once, when my father was looking for my mother, he saw a car that was the same color and make as hers, but it was going in the other direction. He said he made a U-turn and chased the car, but he got pulled over for speeding before he could find out if it was her car or not.

★

I'm not sure how long my mother stayed away the first time she separated from my father. However long that was, she became afraid of being alone and she went back home to him. My father helped my mother move back into their house and they started going to marriage counseling. My sister and I didn't know about any of this when it happened—only what our mother and then our father told us afterward.

★

I was surprised when I found out my father had agreed to attend marriage counseling with my mother. It didn't fit anything I understood about him.

I don't know if my father was afraid to lose my mother, afraid other people would know his marriage had failed, afraid to be alone—or some combination of these fears. Maybe my mother separating from him made my father realize he might die alone.

★

During this time, my mother and my father took a vacation to Hawaii. It is the only time I ever remember them taking a trip together. I remember seeing lots of lush photographs of the island they stayed on, but I don't remember them being in any of the photographs.

★

The other thing about the trip: My father bought two seats on the airplane for himself and one for my mother. My father never said so, but I think that flight was too embarrassing for him. He never flew on an airplane again.

★

My father didn't come to my wedding because he was uncomfortable with the idea of being a fat man in New York City. He didn't want to fly on an airplane—and he was worried about taking cabs, walking down a crowded sidewalk, the size of the hotel rooms.

My father never told me any of that, but my sister did. She wanted me to have some kind of an explanation. Regardless, the fact that my father wasn't there was both an affront and a relief.

★

I don't know if anything happened between my parents on that vacation to Hawaii. I don't know much about what happened between my mother and my father after I wasn't living in their house anymore. I only saw them on special occasions—when there wasn't enough time for things to go too wrong.

★

I also don't know what my parents talked about in marriage counseling. I never asked my father and my mother refuses to talk about it. She doesn't want me to think any more badly of my father than I already do. Of course, I have to assume she was telling me something by not telling me anything. Things must have been worse than I knew.

★

My mother said my father complained about the kitchen being too blue and her cooking making him fat. He told her she didn't make enough money and she was too stupid to balance the checkbook. He told her she wasn't home enough and she wanted to go out too much. My father blamed her for the fact that he didn't have any clean neckties even though they were all stained with food he had spilled on them. He complained about the fifteen pounds she had gained even though she was still skinny. My father complained about her few gray hairs and said her new eyeglasses made her look old. He told her to go on a diet, get contacts, and dye her hair. He told her she was too wrinkly and saggy and dried up. He asked her if gravity and time were angry with her.

★

I just remembered something about our family dinners. There were never any leftovers. My father would eat any food left on the table, any food left on anybody's plate. Then he would complain that we were making him fat. He told us we didn't know how to finish our dinners.

★

My mother said that late in their marriage my father didn't come to bed at night anymore. She said he mostly ate, slept, watched television, and sat on the toilet. She said his snoring had gotten louder and his messed up blood sugar had made him even meaner.

My mother said she wanted to be able to walk through a room without being slapped or hit. My mother said she wanted to go places now that my sister and I were out of the house, but my father didn't want to leave the house much anymore.

★

I don't know how long my mother and my father went to marriage counseling. It may have only been for a couple of weeks, but I was surprised to learn how difficult this was for my father. Apparently, the idea of going to marriage counseling was so upsetting he would get physically sick on the mornings before these counseling appointments—chest pains and headaches and stomachaches, vomiting and diarrhea. Those physical reactions became so bad my father had to take those days off from work, and, eventually, he refused to go with my mother anymore.

★

I like that he suffered that way.

★

When my mother moved out of their house for the second time, she packed boxes and wrapped furniture. She hired movers and scheduled them for a day my father wouldn't be at home. She took half of everything that could be divided up and took everything that could have reminded my father of her—anything that was hers, anything she bought for the house, anything she put on the walls, any of the food she liked, even any of the clothes she bought for him. My father told me it looked like somebody had robbed the house, but didn't want any of his stuff.

★

My father didn't look for my mother the second time she left him. That hadn't worked the first time and he wasn't going to try anymore. He knew she wasn't coming back.

★

After they were divorced, my father would call my mother and propose to her over the telephone. Then he would start laughing and hang up.

★

My mother and my father divorced after thirty-five years of marriage. Sometimes, I wonder if those letters my mother's roommate stole didn't somehow overpower their judgment about each other. Maybe that situation made their relationship something it wasn't. Maybe what happened made them insist on each other when they should have chosen other people.

★

After they divorced, my parents sold the family house they had lived in for most of their marriage, the house my sister and I mostly grew up in. They split up the money and then they each bought their own houses.

My father's new house was a lot like the one they sold, but in a different neighborhood. My mother's house was smaller and closer to where she grew up.

★

When I saw both of them in their new houses, they both seemed diminished. There was so much that was unfinished. In my mother's house, the rooms were mostly empty and there wasn't anything up on the walls. At my father's house, nothing was put away and the backyard was just dirt and mud.

★

After the divorce, my father encountered a kind of loneliness that seemed to quiet him. He said he would go home and nobody would be there and he wouldn't know what to do. He said he would walk through his new house and check all the rooms because he couldn't believe there really wasn't anybody living there with him.

My father's voice got softer and, for a time, he wasn't as mean. He called me on the telephone more often and seemed to want people to like him. It caught me off-guard and made me feel sorry for him even though I still didn't like him.

★

My father always kept guns in the house when I was growing up—a .30-30 Winchester rifle and a 12-gauge shotgun—and, after the divorce, he asked my sister to buy him a handgun. She was living in Florida at the time and it was supposed to be easier to buy handguns there. My sister asked him why he wanted one, but he wouldn't answer her, which made her assume that our father was thinking of killing our mother.

My sister refused to buy our father the handgun and she called our mother to warn her. My mother refused to take any precautions. She said she wasn't afraid of him anymore.

★

Once, my mother told me how my father tried to break into her house. It was late at night and she had just turned off the lights and gone to bed. She heard what sounded like an old pickup truck drive down her quiet side street, which reminded her of my father, which made her get out of bed and peek out the window. My mother turned a corner of a curtain back and saw my father's pickup truck parked across the street. She could see the largeness of my father sitting in the cab and looking at her house. She said he let out a big sigh, which was kind of scary. She said it seemed final somehow. My father got out of his pickup truck and walked toward her house.

★

My mother said my father couldn't walk very well and he stopped when he got to the big oak tree in her front yard and rested there. My father still hadn't seen her, but he had gotten too close to where she was hiding. She said she crouched down on the bedroom floor and didn't move. She said she pretended to not be there.

★

My mother listened as my father opened the screen door on the side of the house and then tried the doorknob. She said the whole house shook and she thought my father was trying to push the door in. Then the house stopped shaking and it got quiet. The screen door closed and latched, but she still didn't move. She said she was afraid to look until she heard my father pull the door of the pickup truck closed and the engine start up. She waited until she heard my father's pickup truck drive away before she got back into bed. She said she didn't know what my father would have done if he had gotten inside her house.

★

After my parents divorced, my father still came to family gatherings at my mother's house around the holidays. I have never understood why my mother and my father couldn't be like regular divorced parents and just have two Thanksgivings, two Christmases, etc.

★

Also, back then, I was still afraid of my father and I sometimes worried that one of our family holidays would end up on the local evening news—one of those stories where the father kills the family and then kills himself. I know this wasn't likely, but my father's loneliness and his guns made it seem possible.

CHAPTER 22

THE TELEVISION WAS on when my father died and I feel a strange need to know the last show he was watching—or at least what channel the television was on. I can't explain this need, but I feel like it is a key piece of information that would help me understand my father.

★

After my father died, my sister started to notice strange things happening around her. For instance, after the memorial service, my sister went home, walked into her living room, and found the television on and the ceiling fan turning overhead. Then, inexplicably, both machines turned off. She is sure that she turned everything off before she left the house, so both parts of this story are difficult to explain.

★

Also, the television was tuned in to a channel that showed old movies, Westerns—something my father would have chosen to watch, but my sister and her family never would have. Also, she swears she noticed the smell of my father in the living room and, after that, she started to notice his smell in places he had never been—in her new car, in a '50s diner just off the highway, in the women's bathroom at her work. I asked my sister whether it was scary and she said the smell was a reassuring presence.

★

Something else: At night, when she couldn't sleep, my sister thought she could hear my father's labored breathing.

★

Not long after my father died, my sister felt compelled to adopt a dog. She had never wanted a dog before, but she couldn't stop thinking about getting one. Eventually, my sister went to the pound and adopted a stray dog that was going to be put down. She was told the dog had been abandoned by a family moving out of the country, but it had papers. It turned out the dog was born on the day my father probably died. The dog was a female, but she named it Ray anyway. My sister was always his favorite, so it makes sense that he came back to her like that.

★

Not long ago, I asked my sister if she still hears from our father, but she hasn't since she had to put the dog down a couple of years ago. Something had changed in the dog and she kept trying to bite my sister, her husband, and their two kids.

★

After my father died, it felt like he was still here but invisible. I could sense his presence. Sometimes, it felt like he was standing in front of me and I couldn't see around him. Other times, it felt like he was pushing down on me and trying to hold me there.

★

I don't know if my sister remembers what I remember. We were haunted by him in different ways.

★

The day after my father's memorial, my last day back in Michigan, I played poker with some of my old friends from high school. We played tournament style, no limit hold'em. I bought in for myself and for my father.

We kept an empty chair at the poker table and an open beer in his cup holder. We dealt him cards and I folded each hand for him. I threw in poker chips for my father each time the blinds came around the poker table until he didn't have any chips left.

★

After my father died, I felt like I was the only person with a dead father. But then I remembered my sister has a dead father too. And then I started to remember all the other dead fathers of people I have known. Tom McMahon's father died when we were ten years old. Ian Brinkman's father died when we were in sixth grade. Bess Simpson's father died while driving to pick her up at the airport over the winter break during our sophomore year in college. Lois Van Epps, her father died in an airplane crash. Jim Young, his father died of leukemia. Donna Tepper's father died from a massive heart attack and Doug Wheeler's father died from a brain aneurysm. Jenny Messing's father died two months before my father died, but the family had known he was going to die for years. They were happy he had lived as long as he did.

★

I didn't know it until my father died, but there is a kind of dead dads club for everybody who has a dead father. There isn't an initiation and you don't get to choose to be in the club. You just are in the club—and you are a different person because of it.

★

One of the things I didn't expect about the dead dads club is the jokes some people with dead dads tell. This is especially true for people whose fathers died before they should have, which is nearly everybody with a father.

★

What's funnier than a dead dad? A dead dad in a clown costume.

How do you make a dead dad float? Two scoops of ice cream, one scoop of dead dad.

How do you make a dead dad float? Take your foot off his neck.

★

At first, I couldn't laugh at the dead dad jokes, but then I started to imagine my actual dead father in the jokes, which made me feel better about the fact that he really had been my father.

★

What's sicker than driving over a dead dad? Skidding over him.

What gurgles and spits up and then shits itself? A dead dad.

★

What's the difference between a dead dad and an onion? You don't cry when you chop up a dead dad.

What's the difference between a dead dad and a styrofoam cup? A dead dad doesn't harm the atmosphere when you burn it.

★

The whole time I was back in Michigan, it felt like my father was dying over those few days. It felt like he was dying on each of those days. The day I left, it felt like he was dead.

CHAPTER 23

MY FATHER RETIRED from the Accident Fund in 2001, which was the earliest date he could start drawing on his pension and his social security. I don't think he ever wanted to work and he quit as soon as he could. The job gave him a watch, a pen, and a retirement party. He said he went home drunk that Friday night and slept in for the weekend.

★

For the next year, my father watched television most nights and slept in most days. Sometimes, he went to the grocery store or out to eat. Other times, he went to his brother's house and they played cards together. A few times, he went to a casino in Mount Pleasant and played in the poker tournaments there. Once, he went on a hunting trip in Northern Michigan and, another time, he went on a fishing trip up there.

★

Besides Stanley Rogan, the only other person who was his friend was his brother, Walter. They fixed cars together and played cards together. They watched porn together and went to strip clubs together. My uncle had a cabin on a lake and they would go up there together. They would take the boat out and fish. It reminded them of something from their childhood.

★

I never felt like my father's friend. Sometimes, I didn't even feel like his son.

★

Even though my father had been a large man for most of his adult life, he got a lot bigger after he retired—getting up to 350 pounds and then over 400 pounds. He looked like he had ballooned each time I saw him. There wasn't any more talk of diets or exercise or anything like that. It seemed like my father had decided to go out however he wanted.

★

There are medical categories for how much people weigh—underweight, healthy weight, overweight (sometimes referred to as pre-obese), obese, morbidly obese, and super obese. Morbidly obese always seemed like the right term for my father—even though *morbidly* just means pathological in this sense. But my father was actually super obese. It was the thing he was best at, being large.

★

This first year after my father retired, I started to talk with him more. We mostly talked about daily things—a movie one of us saw or if he caught any fish, a book I was writing or a poker tournament he played in, the things I was doing to fix up the old house my wife and I had bought or his health problems—but sometimes I would remember something about my childhood, and sometimes he would remember something about his life or a family story I had never been told. It made me feel like I might find out something important about my father, something that might be a key to explaining why he was the way he was. I thought he might tell me something that might let me forgive him.

★

In spite of the fact that I didn't like my father, I had decided I wanted to get to know him better and develop some kind of an adult relationship with him—not father/son, but man/man. I had just moved out of New York City, weighed over 230 pounds, and was learning to take care of myself again. My weight scared me. I didn't want to grow into some version of my father.

★

Today, I am 6'2" tall, a fit 190 pounds.

★

Once, I asked my father about gastric bypass surgery, and he said he had talked with his doctor about it, but he was told he wasn't a good candidate for the surgery. I didn't understand how that could be the case, but my father said he was too big and needed to lose weight before he had the surgery. He was angry with me for making him explain that, so I didn't ask him anything else about it.

*

When I think about this, I realize I learned how to be angry from my father. That's another thing I don't like about him.

*

I just looked up gastric bypass surgery and found out it actually fails for people who can't give up high sugar and high fat foods. I think my father must have known this and lied to me about not being a good candidate for the surgery. I think my father chose Coca-Cola, ice cream, fried fish, potato chips, chili dogs, French fries, and cooking everything with butter over staying alive.

*

Another possibility is that my father was afraid of having the surgery. I might not have that right, but his fears were something I never understood about him. He wouldn't talk about them, but he was afraid of a lot of things—including swimming, diving boards, heights, bridges, mice, dogs, blood, horror movies, horses, his mother (everybody was). It is strange to see that kind of fear on the face of a man so large.

★

After the divorce, I didn't expect my father to remarry or even have another relationship with a woman. It was difficult to think of another woman looking at him and being attracted to him. It was difficult to think of another woman talking to him and liking him. That's why I was surprised when my father started mentioning a woman who worked at the deli counter in the grocery store where he shopped. Apparently, she would joke with him as she sliced the meats and cheeses extra thin for him. He said the deli counter woman made his mouth water, but it was probably the little tastes of the salted meats she gave him while he waited.

★

One day in the summer of 2002, my father and his brother had an argument. It happened while they were doing something in my uncle's garage—my aunt and one of my cousins heard the yelling—but nobody knows what the argument was about. My father and his brother did not speak again for the rest of my father's life. My uncle came to my father's memorial service, and I asked him what happened between them, but he just turned around and walked away from me.

CHAPTER 24

ON THE FLIGHT out of Lansing, the airplane was nearly full. There was only one empty seat and it was beside me. I felt like I was flying with my father with me. I felt like I was flying with the absence of my father with me.

★

It was nighttime on the flight from Detroit to Minneapolis. Looking up, I could see a few faint stars. Looking down, I couldn't see any city lights or streetlights. All I could see was the darkness that was holding us up in the air. There weren't any visible signs of human life.

★

On the last flight home, the snack they gave us was a little bag of Lay's potato chips. That made me think of how, after eating dinner, my father would often get a family-size bag of potato chips out of the cupboard, sit down in front of the television, and then eat the whole bag. He did not share. Sometimes, he would fall asleep with his hand in the bag.

★

After my father died, I talked to a doctor about his overeating and she told me my father probably suffered from cravings—high sugar foods, high fat foods—and those cravings were probably tied to emotional triggers. She said my father probably wasn't even hungry most of the time he binged, but the act of eating must have been comforting for him. She said overeating probably gave him some kind of satisfaction or it might have been a little bit of relief from all his anger.

★

The doctor told me my father's body probably felt terrible when he binged. She said there wasn't enough area in the stomach for that much food and overeating like that stretches the stomach out, which meant my father needed to eat more and more food to feel full.

When she was describing this, I kept thinking of my father as some kind of cartoon character—eating and eating, getting bigger and bigger, until he exploded into little pieces that splattered all over everybody and everything.

★

I don't think my father liked being fat, but I do think he liked being bigger than everybody else.

CHAPTER 25

NOT LONG AFTER my father and his brother stopped talking, my father decided to move to Las Vegas. Within a couple of months, he sold his house—and sold or gave away almost all the belongings he had left from the divorce. He left the family photo albums, any important papers, and crates of beer steins and Coca-Cola memorabilia in my sister's basement.

Then my father packed up his guns, his cowboy boots, his baseball hats, his country music CDs, and all his medications. He packed up his pickup truck with suitcases full of clothes and drove out to Las Vegas. He had always wanted to live there and be a gambler.

★

My father moved to Las Vegas and lived downtown inside a hotel and casino. He paid for his room by the week and he ate his meals at the buffet in the casino. He sent his laundry out to be cleaned and paid for it by the pound. He bought his toiletries and other incidentals in the casino gift shop. He mostly played poker and also some blackjack. My father never said it, but it was clear he didn't think he was going to live much longer.

★

My sister and I didn't think my father was going to live much longer either, so we visited him in Las Vegas and stayed in a hotel room that had a connecting door with the hotel room he lived in. We thought it would be a kind of farewell weekend and he would be dead in a few weeks or a few months.

★

That weekend, we learned about my father's new life in Las Vegas and we did the things he did there. We ate at the breakfast buffet in the morning and the Chinese restaurant on the top floor of the casino at night. We played blackjack during the afternoon and poker after dinner. My father introduced my sister and me to the poker dealers, the pit bosses, and the regulars he played with most days. He seemed proud of us and he was the happiest I had ever seen him.

★

My father really liked Chinese food and I liked to watch him eat it. It made him happy and satisfied in a way that was rare. It felt good to be around him when he was like that.

★

One of the things I noticed that weekend in Las Vegas—it doesn't matter how big you are or what you look like in a casino. If you have money to gamble, people like you.

★

At the airport, before we took our different airplanes home, my sister and I told each other we would visit again in a few months, but neither one of us really thought we would make that trip. We both thought that was the last time we were going to see our father alive.

★

I kept talking to my father on the telephone nearly every day and he didn't die. His various ailments had become less life threatening. He even started to lose some weight and had to buy new clothes. It seemed like he might live for years instead of months or weeks or days. I stopped thinking it was going to be the last time I saw him each time I saw him. I stopped thinking it was going to be the last time I talked with him each time I talked with him.

★

I visited him again a few months later even though my sister couldn't meet me there. I still had this flawed idea that my father and I could somehow become friends—talking about our childhoods and our wives and what we wanted our lives to be. I thought I would learn things about him and about myself. The more I think about my father, the more I think about myself.

★

Of course, it wasn't too long before I realized my father couldn't really talk about himself and I stopped being disappointed with how little I got out of our conversations. Instead, I learned that gambling and eating were two of the few things my father and I had in common. And I learned that I should just do those two things with him while he was alive. I would worry about the rest of it after he was dead.

★

I learned that my father wasn't as mean in Las Vegas as he was in Michigan.

★

There were still little bits of family stories and information that leaked into our conversations. Once, after we had been playing blackjack all night, we were eating these big rib eyes at 5:00 in the morning. My father was talking about the first separation from my mother and how he drove around looking for her. Then he said, "One thing about your mother, she didn't get old like most women her age." That was my father being nice. He meant that she hadn't gotten fat.

★

Another time, after a good run at blackjack, we had colored up and were cashing in our winnings when my father said, "I never liked my dad either. He was the biggest ass-hat."

★

Another time, my father said, "I was glad when my mother died. That meant I didn't have to visit her anymore."

★

Once I was standing at the rail watching my father play no limit Texas hold'em. He had raised the guy who bet and everybody else folded. The hand went all the way to the end and my father overbet the pot. The other guy didn't know what to do and was having a think. At that point, my father turned to me and said, "My dad was fifty-eight years old when he died of natural causes and my mom was sixty-two years old when she died of a heart attack." He said, "I beat them both."

The other guy folded and my father threw his cards into the muck without showing them. The dealer pushed the chips toward my father.

★

Once, we were talking on the telephone and my father mentioned his aunt who was younger than he was. His grandparents had another daughter after his mother gave birth to him. My father told me it was a kind of scandal at the time and his grandparents made his mother take care of his aunt for the first few years of her life.

★

The only thing I remember about my father's aunt was hiding from her and my cousins whenever they showed up at our house. My sister and I were told to get down and my parents would crawl around on the floors locking the doors. We would listen to them knock and try the doorknobs. We would stay on the floor until we heard their car start up and drive away.

★

At some point, I realized I had no idea why we used to hide from my father's aunt and her family. When I asked my father, he told me his aunt was a whore, but then he wouldn't say anything else about it. I don't know what that was supposed to mean or if my father was just fucking with me.

★

On one of my last trips to Las Vegas, my father told me his half sister (the one from his mother's country marriage) got married and had kids who were about the same age as my sister and I. He told me my sister and I once ran against them in a track meet. He didn't tell me if we won and he never told me the family's last name.

★

Once, after catching two blackjacks in a row, my father warned me not to get fat. He said, "You lose inches on your dick."

★

If my father hadn't been my father, I probably never would have talked to him.

*

My trips to Las Vegas to visit my father and talking to him on the telephone felt dutiful. I'm glad I made the attempts, but I also wish I had never tried. It would have been easier to know him less and hate him more.

*

Taking photographs inside a casino is forbidden, but I have one photograph of my father sitting at a poker table. His hair is slicked back like it had been for the last fifty years and he looks massive against the rows of slot machines that light up the background. I don't know who took this photograph.

*

After living a little over a year in Las Vegas, my father decided to go back to Michigan for the summer. His health was pretty bad and he thought it might be the last time he would see everybody. During those few months, my father lived with my sister and her husband and their two kids. Nearly every day of those few months, my sister and her husband fought about my father's overbearing presence in their house and my father pretended their fighting had nothing to do with him. My father knew my sister wouldn't ask him to leave and my sister knew her husband wouldn't leave her.

*

That summer, my father slept most of the day and most of the night on the couch in their living room, even though they had fixed up a guest room for him. The problem was that the guest room was on the second floor of the house and it was difficult for my father to walk up or down a flight of stairs. Whether he was sleeping or not, my father kept the television turned on with the volume turned up high.

★

My father could take up so much space that nobody wanted to be in the room with him.

★

That summer, my father was on a strange diet that included lots of water pills, which were supposed to reduce his body weight by eliminating excess water. My father didn't lose any noticeable weight, but he made a lot of trips to the bathroom. The thing is, when my father took a piss, he often sprayed the bathroom floor around the toilet and, sometimes, the wall next to the toilet. Sometimes, the toilet paper was wet because of this.

I don't know how this is possible, but my father never seemed to realize he was doing this, or, if he did, he never tried to clean up after himself. I suppose admitting it would have also meant admitting he couldn't really reach his dick anymore.

★

My father went back to Las Vegas at the end of the summer, and, after he left, my sister and her husband had to tear out the flooring around that toilet and repaint the wall next to it. They also had to throw out the couch in the living room where my father spent most of his days watching television and sleeping. The fabric was stained with yellow sweat and spilled food. The padding inside the cushions had been flattened and it made them think of my father every time they looked at it. My sister told me buying new living room furniture probably saved their marriage.

★

My father lived for about another year in Las Vegas, but he never expected to live that long. That's part of why he almost ran out of money toward the end of his life and decided to move back to Michigan. The other part of that, I think, is that my father wasn't a very good gambler. He had the odd big win, but one of the things I noticed on my trips to Las Vegas was that he lost pretty consistently.

★

My father never said any of that was why he was moving back to Michigan. He said he wanted to spend time with his grandchildren, and maybe he did, but that's almost always a lie when somebody says it. Also, my father needed somebody to take care of him.

★

My father decided to drive his pickup truck from Las Vegas back to Michigan and Stanley Rogan flew out to Las Vegas to share the driving with him. My father knew he couldn't do it by himself anymore.

*

The second day of the trip back, they got an early start. My father was driving and Stanley was dozing in the passenger seat. It was a bright morning and they were on Interstate 70, somewhere in the middle of Kansas, when my father says he blacked out. He probably fell asleep, but my father never would have described it that way. Regardless, Stanley woke up first and started yelling at my father who then woke up too. By this time, my father had driven off the road and the pickup truck was headed for the ditch between them and the interstate going the other way. My father turned the steering wheel hard, trying to pull them back onto the road, and that sent the pickup truck into a roll.

*

Neither one of them is sure how many times the pickup truck rolled, but, miraculously, they came to a stop with the wheels touching the ground. They were still strapped in by their seat belts (my father's had an extension) and they were even facing east. The motor was still running, so my father put the pickup truck in park and turned to look at Stanley. My father said, "I suppose you want to drive now."

CHAPTER 26

THE DAY AFTER I returned home from my father's memorial service, I heard a loud noise at the front of the house. One of the window-panes was smeared and there was a bird lying on the porch. It was still alive, but breathing hard. I picked it up and set it on its feet. I was hoping it was just stunned and it might fly away.

When I let go of the bird, its neck tipped over and the rest of its body followed. The bird had a broken neck and I didn't know how long it was going to take for it to die. I picked the bird up and held it in my two hands to comfort it. The bird fluttered its wings a little bit and settled down in my hands. It made a tiny chirp, shit and pissed on my hands, then stopped breathing or moving.

★

When I looked up, I noticed another bird watching us from under some of the bushes in front of the house. I took my T-shirt off, spread it out next to the bushes, and placed the dead bird on it. I was trying to make the living bird understand that the dead bird was dead. I sat there with the living bird and it did not fly away. We had a kind of silent memorial service. Then the living bird hopped forward onto my T-shirt, nudged the dead bird with its beak, looked up at me, and flew away.

*

Sometimes, I still want to ask my father some questions about his life or about how he treated my sister and me when we were growing up. Sometimes, I will even say a question out loud just to get it out of my body.

My father still doesn't say anything back. It's just like it was when he was alive.

*

I'm awake and my father is dead. It's snowing and my father is dead. I'm hungry and my father is dead.

*

One of the things I took home with me from my father's apartment was an undeveloped roll of film that I found in a kitchen drawer. I got the roll developed and kind of hoped I would find something revealing on those twenty-four photos. One photograph shows three watches and seven rings. Another photograph shows four necklaces and a pair of cufflinks. Another shows two cell phones. There are three photographs of fishing rods and tackle boxes, three photographs of framed prints he never hung up in his new apartment, and one photograph of a box of CDs. There is one photograph of his .30-30 Winchester rifle, one of his 12-gauge shotgun, and one of the Glock handgun. There is one photograph of the couch, one of the bed, and one of the floor. The other eight photographs are all partially or completely obscured by my father's thumb or fingers.

At first, I couldn't figure out what the photographs were for, but then I realized he took them for his apartment insurance. This was all my father had left and he was afraid of getting robbed and losing it.

★

One of my father's things I couldn't throw away was a blue note-book. I found it on his dining room table and it was full of lined paper that had a different person's name written at the top of each page—his name, my mother's name, my name, my sister's name, the names of his brothers and his sister (but not his half sister), the names of his parents and his grandparents, and the names of relatives I had never met. After each name, each of the lined pages was blank.

★

My father always wanted me to write about him and his side of the family. He bought the blue notebook with the idea that he was going to write down stories he remembered and then tell me about them when we talked on the telephone. My father might tell a different version of this story.

★

I wish that I was making some of this up.

★

On the national news, there was a story about a family on vacation at Disney World. They checked into a hotel and, after they were in their room, the father shot his wife. Then he drowned their two small children in the bathtub. They didn't even get to see Mickey Mouse and Goofy first.

I turned to my wife and said, "I'm glad he wasn't my father." Somehow, that helped.

CHAPTER 27

WHEN MY FATHER moved back to Michigan, my sister found him a one bedroom apartment he could pay for on his social security. He bought a new bed, a new couch, and a new television with some of the money he had left and my sister gave him back the things she had stored for him in her basement while he was in Las Vegas. She helped him with the new apartment—unpacking everything, setting up the telephone and utilities, etc. Our father couldn't do a lot of these things for himself anymore and my sister took on most of this burden.

★

Toward the end of his life, my father had difficulty walking. This was partly because of his weight and partly because he had developed bone spurs on his feet (which were partly caused by his weight). The bone spurs were his feet's response to being asked to carry so much weight. His feet started making extra bone to support the extra pounds. His feet were the only thing trying to do something about my father's weight.

*

My father had different canes and walkers to help him get around, but his difficulty walking meant there were times when my father didn't leave his apartment for days or for weeks. During these times, my father made a list of things he needed—mostly groceries—and my sister bought them, brought them back to his apartment, and put them away for him.

*

Right after my father moved back to Michigan, he started calling me every day and, for a while, I talked with him every day. Without the casino, he didn't have much else to do inside his apartment besides eat and watch television.

Back in Michigan, something changed inside my father and he became really mean again. Usually, the meanness took the form of simple insults and cuts, trying to correct or undercut nearly anything I said, the kind of thing I heard and felt when I was growing up. This time around, though, my father seemed pathetic in a way that allowed me to ignore the fact that the things he said were directed at me. He mostly seemed lonely and answering the telephone seemed like an easy enough way to keep him company.

★

During these telephone calls, my father also started to fall asleep. It didn't matter who was talking. Sometimes, my father would just trail off into a mutter and then I would hear him start snoring. Other times, it would seem like he was interrupting me, but then I would hear him start snoring. The funniest times were when I just heard the telephone hit the floor and then nothing but background noise.

The first few times this happened, I yelled my father's name until he woke up. After a while, I just started hanging up on him. He usually didn't call me back until the next day.

★

My father also started getting confused or maybe hallucinating during some of these telephone conversations. Sometimes, he called me his dead brother's name, Kenny. Other times, he called me his living brother's name, Walter. Every once in a while, he called me by the name of one of my cousins, Butch. It always made me think he wanted a different son.

★

Once, out of nowhere, my father started talking about chili dogs and shotguns. Another time, he started ordering Chinese takeout from me before I interrupted him.

★

Once, my father started yelling, "It's a bear. It's a bear." I tried to talk to him, but there wasn't any response. Then it sounded like he set the telephone down and I heard a loud bang in the background. When my father got back on the telephone, I asked him what happened and he said he made the bear disappear.

★

Eventually, the telephone calls with my father became so frustrating and difficult that I stopped answering the telephone every time he called. I felt guilty about doing this and I felt silly about a simple realization: I wasn't required to talk to my father even if he was my father.

★

The more I didn't answer my father's telephone calls, the more he called. Sometimes, he called dozens of times and I would eventually answer the telephone just so he would stop calling. Unfortunately, that only lasted for the rest of the day—and sometimes he would even forget we had talked in the afternoon and call me again in the evening, telling me the same things he had told me earlier in the day. I can't remember ending any one of these telephone calls with my father and feeling good about it.

★

I did not talk to my father for most of the last year he was alive. I should have stopped talking to him years before, though—it was such a huge relief. I was so much happier not talking with him than I was talking with him. It was a form of self-preservation.

★

I stopped talking to my father, but my father did not stop calling me every day and leaving messages. At first, I listened to the messages, but they were almost always the same: "Danny, this is your father. Call me back."

It was almost always a statement and a command. He was still trying to tell me what to do.

★

I kept not answering his telephone calls. I started erasing the messages without listening to them.

★

At one point, my wife and I considered changing our telephone number. Ironically, that seemed like too mean of a thing to do.

★

Almost a year passed without talking to my father. I felt lighter and I began to feel like I could answer his telephone calls again. Around Christmas in 2004, I picked up the receiver and my father was on the other end of the line. He was surprised I answered the telephone and sounded excited that he caught me. He asked me what I had been up to and I told him I'd been really busy. We never said anything else about it.

★

In one of our last telephone calls, my father told me he had just been to the doctor's office and he had gained a lot of weight. He hadn't used a home scale for years because he couldn't see over his belly to read the numbers between his feet and, even if he could have, the numbers didn't go high enough to measure his weight. For years, my father could only find out how much he weighed at the doctor's office. This last time, though, my father didn't know what the exact number was. He had maxed out the doctor's 500-pound scale. He was bigger than that.

★

Really fat people move in different ways than people who are not really fat. For instance, my father had to stand up in stages. Since he didn't really fit in most chairs or on most couches, he often sat on the floor. To get up, he needed to hold on to something he could push or pull—a door, a chair, or another piece of furniture. Then he would roll over onto his side and up onto his knees while pushing or pulling his upper body up. From his knees, he would get one foot flat on the ground and then the other foot. Then he would straighten his legs up. Once his legs were under him, he could raise his upper body until he was standing upright. Once he was standing, he didn't move for a while. He had to rest and catch his breath.

★

When my father pushed himself up, he didn't do it with an open hand. He did it with a fist. The last time he used an open hand, he dislocated two fingers on his right hand. Nobody's fingers are strong enough to hold up that much weight.

★

My father's arms were always bigger than my legs.

★

My father's legs were really strong just from standing up and walking. Each step he took had to carry his 500+ pounds.

★

The legs of super obese people usually rub together, so they start to throw them out to the side when they walk. Their arms get pushed out to the side by their growing torsos too. Their proportions start to resemble the proportions of a baby—except that with super obese people, the head is a really small part of their body.

★

Almost any obese person looks hunched. My father looked a little deformed with all that weight pushing down on him. He must have wanted to push himself out of that body.

★

Also, the arms of any obese person seem to be too short. Sometimes, I watched my father reach out for objects and then be a little baffled when his hands didn't get there. It must have seemed like an optical illusion, those objects moving farther away from him.

★

As my father got older, his hair started to turn gray, but it just made him seem more and more blond. Plus, his face never seemed to get any wrinkles. As he got bigger and fatter, his skin just seemed to get taut, which made my father look younger than he was.

★

There is a late photograph of my father driving a speedboat. The sunlight is on his face and the wind is in his hair. His grandson is sitting on his lap and my sister is sitting next to them, her daughter on her lap.

It looks like everybody is smiling, but they might just be squinting. It is difficult to be certain. It is toward the end of the day and the sun is setting outside the frame of the photograph.

★

After we started talking again, my father started calling me every day again. The last telephone call I received from my father, he left his usual message. I didn't call him back because I knew he would call again later or call again the next day.

★

My father didn't call the next day and I remember wondering about it that night. I thought there might be something wrong with him, but then I forgot about it for a couple of days.

★

My father didn't call me on my birthday either and I thought there might be something wrong with him, but it was my birthday and I didn't want to deal with it right then. It was a relief when my father didn't call for a while.

★

I don't feel guilty for not talking to my father for that year, but I do feel guilty about not calling him back that one time. There were so many times I thought my father was going to die soon, but he didn't die any of those times. I started to think he was just going to get bigger and bigger and keep living and all that size was somehow going to protect him from death.

★

I want to talk to my father again now that he is dead.

★

Once, I dialed my father's old telephone number just to see if he really was dead. Somehow, it seemed possible he might answer. There was a recording saying the number had been disconnected. The recording said no other information was available for his number.

★

The last photograph I have of my father is probably from a couple of months before he died. My sister probably took the shot because I don't think he would have let anybody else photograph him in this position. My father is lying on the living room floor— kind of on his side and also kind of on his back. His head is hanging at an awkward angle—held up off the floor by his neck fat. His mouth is hanging open. He's probably just sleeping, but it could have been a photograph of him dead.

CHAPTER 28

THERE IS SOMETHING I haven't been able to say yet. For most of my life, I have been trying to forget about it, and I've been afraid to write it down, but I have to include it here or this will not be finished.

★

This is what would happen: Sometimes, if my mother left my sister and me alone with my father, he would take my sister into my parents' bedroom and give her money for doing things. He would give her a nickel to take off his socks and shoes. He would give her a dime to unbutton his shirt. He would give her a quarter to unbuckle his belt. She got another quarter to pull his pants off by their legs and another one to slide his underwear down his hips and his legs.

★

My father never closed the bedroom door all the way during these sessions and I could see them in my parents' bed. I could hear my father talking softly to my sister, giving her instructions. She never said much while this was happening. She just did what he asked her to do.

★

My father gave her a fifty-cent piece to kiss his butt and another one to hold on to his testicles, one of them in each of her small hands. She got a silver dollar for pulling his foreskin back until the head popped out.

It looked huge in both of her small hands. It was too big for her to put it in her mouth, but sometimes he would give her another silver dollar to lick it.

★

As a little boy, I thought my sister was getting rich, but I also knew something was wrong. I didn't understand enough of what was happening to explain it.

★

I don't know how many times my father did that to my sister, but, once, I opened the bedroom door, walked into my parents' bedroom, and said I wanted to do it too. I didn't really want to do it, but I wanted my father to stop doing that to my sister. I also wanted the money my father was giving to my sister.

★

My father said he would give me a silver dollar if I put it in my mouth. I didn't want to do it, but I did want the silver dollar, which is probably why I bit down on it really hard when I did it. It was a tricky thing being a little kid in that kind of situation—wanting the money but knowing there was something wrong with what was happening.

★

When I bit him, my father screamed and hit me really hard on the side of the head. I remember stumbling off to the side and trying to not fall down. I can still hear my ears ringing and feel how wobbly everything went after that.

★

When my mother came home from wherever she was, I told her my father had been bad. She says she asked me what he had done and I said he had been really bad. Apparently, I couldn't explain what happened—or she didn't want to understand what I was saying.

I don't remember that part of it. She told me that after he died.

★

I don't remember it happening again with my sister or with me after that, but I don't know how something like that stops.

★

Sometimes, I wonder if my memory is faulty, if things didn't actually happen like this, but then I remember the time I found these incest magazines in my father's closet. I was looking for regular porn, but found these magazines with stories and photos of fathers and daughters, mothers and sons, aunts and uncles and cousins.

★

Once, my mother asked me how I could still talk to my father after the things he had done to me growing up and I told her I just ignored all that. That was an easy answer, but it felt like it allowed me to be a different person than the one who those things happened to.

★

Also, there is such a strong pull to like your father and your mother whether you want to or not—and I really wanted to like my father. I wanted to not blame him. I wanted to forgive him. I wanted to be one of the people in the world who actually likes their father.

★

I hated my father whether I talked to him on the telephone or not. I hated my father whether I saw him or not.

★

I don't really understand how my sister and I could still see our father after the things he did to each of us. There were the things he did to me and the things he did to her. We experienced those things separately, but they connected us in a way that is difficult to understand. My sister and I don't talk about what happened. Sometimes, I hope she has somehow blocked it all out even though I haven't forgotten.

★

Before my father died, I felt like everybody lived in a certain relation to everybody else. I imagined everybody who I knew on a map with lines drawn in to connect us all. Now everybody feels unconnected and everything feels uncertain.

★

My sister and I lived through our childhoods together, but different things happened to us. Even now, seeing each other reminds us of that.

★

My sister is morbidly obese and seeing her now reminds me of my father. Her body has gotten fat in some of the ways my father's body did. I see my father in the way the soft fat moves on her upper arms. I see my father in the way the fleshy jowls droop below her lower jaw. I try to ignore this. I try to push these thoughts out of my head. I want to get my father out of me.

★

The walls look different now that my father is dead. They look like they could fall down and they never did before.

★

Sometimes, I look at the empty space around me and feel like my father is invisible and still surrounding me.

★

Being our father was not an excuse.

CHAPTER 29

I AM NOT a father.

★

I've been using *father* all through this because it seemed right—also, because it gave me some distance—but I never called him my father. I never called him Father. I called him Dad.

★

This is everything I have to say about my father.

★

If you take the *e* out of *dead*, you get *dad*.

★

My sister didn't want anything to do with our dad's ashes and I almost left them with the funeral home. They would have eventually thrown them away after enough time had passed.

★

When I got home with my dad's ashes, I put them up on a high shelf in the garage. I wasn't going to let my dad in the house.

★

I didn't know what to do with my dad's ashes—bury them in a grave, pour them into an urn, spread them out over some body of water, shoot them up into the sky and explode them in fireworks, leave them on a shelf in the garage and forget about them.

★

I decided to take my dad's ashes back to Las Vegas for one last trip. I bought two tickets for the flight there—one for me and one for my dad's ashes.

★

My dad's ashes weighed just over six pounds, which means he lost around 500 pounds after he died.

★

I started talking to his ashes. I started calling the ashes Dad.
"Dad, we're getting on the airplane."
"Dad, you can have the window seat."
"Dad, I'm putting your seat belt on for you."

★

When the airplane landed, my dad's ashes jostled and shifted in his box. It seemed like he was excited to get downtown, get checked in to the Plaza, and get down to the tables.

★

Up in the hotel room, I held my dad up to the window and showed him the skyline of Las Vegas. I said, "Dad, what do you want to do first—gamble or eat?"

★

I took my dad to Binion's, bought into a no limit hold'em game there, and sat down with my dad in the one seat. Between hands, under the poker table, I opened the box with my dad's ashes in it and sprinkled a little bit of him on the floor of the poker room. I thought they would vacuum the carpet later, so I stepped on my dad with my shoes and worked as much of him into the carpet as I could.

★

I cashed in our poker chips for a small win and walked my dad over to El Cortez to play blackjack. I sat down at third base and sat my dad down on the stool next to mine. I played two hands—one for him and one for me—and during one of the shuffles, I sprinkled little bits of my dad around the bottom of the blackjack table. I watched him disappear into a deep seam of the carpet there.

★

I started talking to my dad about what we should do with certain blackjack hands.

Dad, do you want to hit your hard sixteen?

Dad, he's got an ace up. Should we take insurance?

Dad, you should split those eights.

Dad, I'm going to double down.

★

My dad and I were both up big when one of the pit bosses told me we couldn't play blackjack there anymore. He said the dealer would color us up and we could play any other game in the casino, just not blackjack.

★

It was getting late and I was getting hungry and I'm sure my dad was too. I picked my dad up and took him to the cashier's window. We cashed out our wins and went outside to see what time it was.

We had lost time inside the casino and it was almost daylight. I decided my dad wanted to try the new breakfast buffet at the Golden Nugget.

★

I bought two tickets for the all-you-can-eat breakfast buffet, which was confusing to the cashier, but I didn't try to explain it. I grabbed a booth for us and set my dad down on one side. I loaded up plates of food for both of us—pancakes, bacon, and sausage, lots of maple syrup. I ate all my breakfast and went back for seconds. I left all my dad's food uneaten on the other side of the booth.

★

I took my dad back to the Plaza and the elevators weren't working, so I carried him up the flights of stairs to our hotel room. He got heavy.

★

Inside the room, I opened the window up to let some dry air in and noticed there wasn't a window screen. I opened the box of my dad up and, for the first time, noticed the little bits of bone in his ashes.

★

I decided to dump my dad out the window overlooking Las Vegas. It was windy outside and some of his ashes blew back into my face. Little bits of my dad got stuck to my face and my hands. My dad was gritty and he tasted chalky. I watched a little cloud of my dad puff up and then disappear into the wind. I thought I heard little bits of my dad clatter against the front of the hotel as I scattered him over downtown Las Vegas.

★

I closed the window and threw the box that had held my dad inside it into the trash. I walked into the bathroom and washed my dad off my face and my hands. I opened some mouthwash and rinsed my dad out of my mouth. I spit in the sink.

★

Sometimes, I say, "I love you anyway." I can only say it now because I know he can't hear me.

*

I tie my shoes in the morning and my dad is dead. It's lunchtime and my dad is dead. I get the mail and my dad is dead. It's sunny outside and my dad is dead. I'm happy right now and my dad is dead.

*

Everything I do now, I do it with a dead dad.

A NOTE ON THE AUTHOR

Michael Kimball is the author of *The Way the Family Got Away, How Much of Us There Was, Dear Everybody* and his novels have been translated into a dozen languages. His work has been featured on NPR's *All Things Considered*, and in the Guardian, *Vice, Bomb*, and *New York Tyrant*. He is also responsible for the project Michael Kimball Writes Your Life Story (on a postcard) and a couple of documentary films. Visit his website at www.michael-kimball.com.